House of Fish

Jonah

House of Fish
Jonah

Ilana Harris

Published by Mosaica Press, Inc.
www.mosaicapress.com
info@mosaicapress.com

Any great undertaking comes with fear. Often we fear failure. Sometimes we even fear success. Are we worthy of it? Can we sustain it? We long for the security of the familiar, the life we have known. We are afraid of the unknown, the uncharted territory...

There is no way back.
There is only a way forward.

Rabbi Jonathan Sacks

Table of Contents

Preface IX

Acknowledgments XI

Chapter 1: The Prophecy 1

Chapter 2: Running Away 6

Chapter 3: Tarshish 9

Chapter 4: The Parting 12

Chapter 5: The King 18

Chapter 6: The Boat 22

Chapter 7: The Storm 28

Chapter 8: The Lottery 33

Chapter 9: Overboard 39

Chapter 10: The Sailors 44

Chapter 11: The Fish 49

Chapter 12: A Second Time 55

Chapter 13: Nineveh 61

Chapter 14: Nineveh's Response 66

Chapter 15: Nineveh Repents 73

Chapter 16: Kikayon 78

Chapter 17: The Worm 84

Author's Notes 89

Glossary. 100

Educator's Guide. 101

Bibliography 103

Preface

*A*ll too often, the biblical book of Jonah is overlooked, both because of its brevity, at just forty-eight verses long, as well as overfamiliarity. Exposure from a young age has fooled some of us into assuming we already know the story and have little to learn or gain from another reading.

Years of teaching Jonah showed me that this couldn't be further from the truth. *Jonah: House of Fish* grew out of my passion and enthusiasm for the fascinating and profound story of Jonah, as well as my desire to share that with you.

This novel was written to provide an immersive experience into the biblical period, allowing readers to engage with Jonah while staying true to classic and contemporary sources. Wherever possible, I have relied on these sources and included them at the back of the book for your perusal. To that end, I consulted those wiser and more knowledgeable than myself, but the responsibility for all mistakes lies with me. I assumed poetic license for topics lacking source material, such as the identity of Jonah's wife and the origin of Jonah's money.

This book highlights the many layers of wisdom contained within the Book of Jonah—not just the numerous parallels within the four chapters, but also the many other biblical stories woven into the text. It also showcases the central figure in the story, Jonah. This prophet is a champion and advocate for the Israelites, a man willing to sacrifice himself for the sake of his people.

By spotlighting numerous issues from which Jonah, and we, are meant to learn, the book of Jonah provides much inspiration for our own lives. Lessons range from tolerance, change, appreciating the Divine plan, and social responsibility.

As Abraham Joshua Heschel writes, "Jonah is running to Tarshish, whilst Nineveh is tottering on the brink. Are we not all guilty of Jonah's failure?"[1]

---

1   Heschel, *Moral Grandeur*, p. 292, cited by Brown, xxxviii.

Acknowledgments

Thanks to the Almighty, without Whom none of this would have been possible.

Thank you to my students for keeping me on my toes, prompting me to delve ever deeper to find fresh insights into Jonah.

I am grateful to my teachers for sparking my own interest in learning. Heartfelt gratitude to one of my mentors, Rabbanit Shani Taragin, who continues to teach me so much. She encouraged me from the start and has been so generous with her time.

With thanks to Rabbi Yaacov Haber and Rabbi Doron Kornbluth, who met my manuscript with immediate enthusiasm. The two of them, together with their dedicated team, in particular Miri, brought this book to life.

Thanks to Rabbi Johnny Solomon for his insightful comments, and Rav Yoni Rosensweig for helping me find elusive sources. Thanks to Rabbi Dr. Raphael Zarum for his thought-provoking ideas on Jonah and Assyria. In addition, I had two wonderful tour guides for the Ancient Assyrian collections. Rebbetzin Shoshana Tugendhaft of the British Museum in London was always readily available to answer my queries on the subject. Nachliel Selavan of the Israel Museum, Jerusalem, was very helpful in providing me with details about life in ancient Assyria.

I have deep appreciation for the support I received from Jemma Jacobs, along with her suggestions and edits. Nadia Jacobson and Batnadiv Hakarmi provided me with the tools to craft this book, as well as the inspiration to form a writing group. My group provided me with ongoing encouragement and feedback, and put up with hearing about Jonah over and over again.

Thank you to my family and friends, champions and supporters, and to my beta readers: Mum, Rebecca, and Esther. My husband, Shmuel, has been my rock, reading drafts and cheering me on. My wonderful children hope that this book will make me famous, or at least ensure I can provide some interesting bedtime stories...

Chapter 1

The Prophecy

The circle of dancers wove in and out.

Jonah's arms swung up and down with gusto, and his head nodded along to the tune. He tapped his legs in time to the beat, his steps synchronized with theirs. It was difficult to spot his feet among the jigging and kicking of his neighbors as their frantic movements stirred up small clouds of dust.

Jonah clutched the men next to him in a tight embrace, oblivious to the damp sweat and stale odors that hung over the crowd. His own tunic was plastered to his back, soaking wet from hours of jubilant dancing.

As Jonah and his neighbors swayed in unison, he experienced intense feelings of connection with and love for all the people around him. He threw back his head and laughed with exuberance. His joy was infectious, and those around him smiled and cheered aloud, feeling emboldened to sing louder and with more passion and fervor.

Jonah marveled at this opportunity to celebrate the water-drawing ceremony with Israelites from all walks of life. He was so grateful that he and Shoshana had been able to come to the Temple. He just wished they could have brought some of the other villagers with them.

He scooped up his four species. Having danced with them earlier on, he had placed them on the side for safekeeping throughout the celebrations. He cradled the bundle of date palm, willow, and myrtle in his right hand, admiring the golden thread used to tie them together, a local Jerusalem custom. In his left hand he clutched the fragrant lemon-like citrus fruit, known as an etrog.

Bringing his hands close, he merged the four species together, enjoying the rustling noise they made as he gently shook them. He hugged

1

them close, grateful that he could once again fulfill this commandment during the week of Sukkot.

The four species were especially meaningful to him, as each symbolized a different type of Israelite and their varying levels of knowledge and observance. This ranged from the willow, with neither fragrance nor taste, symbolizing a person with neither good deeds nor Torah learning; to the etrog, with its fine taste and fragrance, representing a person with both. The commandment to gather all four species in one bundle taught that the people of Israel, too, need to be united, regardless of their differences.

Jonah took a pause from the festivities to gaze at his surroundings. Positioned on the fifteen wide steps leading up to the Temple entrance, the band of Levites played their instruments with great skill and devotion. Flutes, harps, lyres, trumpets, bells, and the loud beat of the drums could all be heard.

The area was ablaze with light shining from the four golden lamps. The whole of Jerusalem was illuminated by the oil from these towering candelabras, giving the illusion that it was daytime rather than the middle of the night.

It was breathtaking to watch the young and agile priests swiftly climb up the thick ropes to reach the lamps, balancing the lit torches in their hands and mouths. There were gasps from the ladies gathered in the women's section as a young priest somersaulted from one rope to the next, performing a multitude of impressive acrobatics.

Talented priests stood alongside wise and learned sages, all of them tossing fire-lit sticks into the air, casting more light on the scene. Children watched, mesmerized by the daring displays of juggling and gymnastics. Their arms waved in the air as they tried to mimic the complex movements, and they clapped their hands in amusement and glee.

He craned his neck to catch a glimpse of his wife, Shoshana, in the crowd of women. He caught sight of her face, radiant with joy. He smiled at her childlike delight and enthusiasm. Even now, after their many years together, he felt such gratitude to have her as his partner.

Jonah breathed in deeply, and the scent of freshly cooked meat from the sacrifices entered his nostrils. The tantalizing smells were tempting, generating in him quite an appetite. He had seen some lads eating pieces of meat threaded on sticks, the dark juice dripping down their chins. He noticed a stall serving bowls of vegetable soup. Clusters of children walked around with sticky fingers dipping into bags of almonds and dried apricots.

The smell of freshly baked bread from the *Lechem Hapanim* was heavenly. As he moved further along the courtyard, he caught an intense whiff of the *Ketoret*, the intoxicating incense. This potent mix of eleven herbs and spices gave off an ethereal fragrance that was heady to smell and had the power to raise a person's consciousness, allowing one to transcend to celestial levels.

As Jonah experienced these heightened senses and enlightened state, he found himself growing giddy and faint. He realized that he was about to have a seizure, a sign of an impending prophetic revelation. Stepping away from the crowd, he looked around for Shoshana, in need of her assistance. Realizing that he wouldn't find her in time, he quickly leaned his back against a nearby wall. Then he crouched down with his head between his knees just as dizziness overtook him and the prophetic state overcame him.

When he came to, Jonah was curled in a fetal position on the ground. He breathed in slowly and deeply, allowing himself time to adjust and regain his normal state of consciousness. The words of God echoed loudly in his head.

It had been a short message, commanding him, "Arise. Go to Nineveh, that great city, and call out against it, for their wickedness has come before me." His task was to deliver this prophecy and elicit a response of repentance. His mind felt foggy and clouded. Grating noise reverberated through his aching head. Jonah sighed irritably as he massaged his temples. The slow circular motion provided only mild relief from his pain.

He was uncertain how long he had been immersed in prophecy. It was still bright outside. He couldn't be sure whether that was an indication of daytime or if the oil lamps were still alight. His eyes seemed to swim in and out of focus, and details appeared blurry, with people looking like fuzzy shadows.

Jonah stumbled to his feet like a drunk man waking from a stupor. His head was throbbing, and his body was shaking. He lurched forward. The palm of his hand desperately groped for the wall as he leaned in for physical stability as well as the reassurance that he was back in reality. The feel of the cold stone against his clammy hand helped to ground him. He pressed his forehead against the wall, shutting his eyes to block out the foggy images.

I can't do this again, he thought. This was not a prophecy he was willing to bear. He was well aware of the severe punishment of death for a prophet who didn't deliver his message, but Jonah couldn't contemplate carrying out this mission. Merely thinking about it sent panic throughout his body.

God's directions had been brief and unclear. His mind hadn't been properly attuned to absorb or interpret the entirety of the Divine message; some parts were still hazy and incomplete. More instructions were waiting, like wisps of smoke floating around his head, just out of reach. He certainly wasn't planning on sticking around to receive the details of the prophecy.

If only it were that easy to erase the words, to dismiss them, like a letter that hasn't found its way. He wished he could forget that God had spoken to Him. If only he could ignore the prophecy and carry on with life as usual.

It hadn't been like this on previous occasions. He hadn't necessarily embraced his earlier prophecies, but he had accepted them. This one, though, turned everything on its head.

He berated himself, wishing for someone on whom he could take out his anger and lay blame. Why had he been so passive? Why hadn't he responded to God, adamantly refusing to follow His directive?

A hollow laugh left his mouth at this ridiculous thought. As if he, a mere mortal standing in the Temple, the holiest place in the world, in the presence of the Creator of the world, would dare do such a thing. He was no Moses, nor a Jeremiah. What would he have said? In any case, what would be the point, when God knew his every thought and reaction. No response would be adequate.

Jonah, the prophet who wove words and spun tales, articulate and eloquent—where were his words now? He was at a complete loss; he couldn't express himself. His wellspring had dried up. God asking this of him had struck him silent.

Chapter 2

Running Away

Jonah hunched over. His weight rested on the stone wall as he allowed himself time to recover. His body was still, frozen in place, but his mind was racing, whirring with thoughts and jumping all over the place. The splitting headache, one of the side effects of receiving a prophecy, didn't help matters.

The prophecy had ignited a fire within him, and now it was roaring and burning with zeal, waiting for him to launch into action. He needed to quiet the fire, douse the flames, and drown out the voice in his head. He had to act, to do something, to get away.

He resented the mission; the people of Nineveh should not be allowed this opportunity for repentance. He must leave the Land of Israel as quickly as possible, before the particulars and specifics of the prophecy were revealed to him. He just hoped that being beyond the physical borders of this holy land would be enough to prevent God from speaking to him again.

Stopping just beyond the Temple grounds, Jonah paused to collect his belongings. Since no leather, metal, nor weapons were allowed in this holy sanctuary, he had left these items with the attendant for safekeeping. He gathered his scuffed leather sandals, silver dagger, and large bag of coins, handing the young man a small coin for the service.

The strong smell of goatskin greeted him. Even with age, it hadn't faded from his bag. The scent didn't bother him as much now as it had when he had first procured it. He slung it over his shoulder. From his purse he extracted his pendant, slipping it over his head and tucking it under his tunic. Then he hid the heavy purse and weapon on his person and wrapped the straps of his sandals around his ankles, securing them tightly.

"Jonah!" a high-pitched voice called to him.

He looked up to see his wife standing in front of him, her sandals already tied, and a small knapsack on her back. Usually, her presence brought a smile to his face and light to his eyes, but not now. Guilt flooded him as he realized that since coming to, in his haste to escape, his mind had been elsewhere.

"What's wrong? Where have you been?" she asked as she kneeled down beside him, her face lined with worry.

"We have to go," he responded brusquely. "I'll tell you on the way." He was trying to push off the conversation because he knew she wouldn't like what he had to say.

With that, he started moving, sprinting in his urgency to leave. His faded sandals slapped against the worn cobblestones as he left the Temple far behind. He could hear Shoshana at his heels, scrambling to keep up with him.

Weaving through the narrow streets, Jonah noticed all the sukkot, the temporary shelters covered with leafy branches. Large and small, these booths, beautifully decorated with fruits and draped with garlands of flowers and palm branches, were occupied by inhabitants of Jerusalem as well as the visiting pilgrims.

As he passed them by, he could hear the sounds of children playing, of families singing and exchanging words of Torah. The enticing smells emanating from the festive meal each family was enjoying reminded him how hungry he was, and his mind turned to more practical issues, like food supplies.

Jonah checked what provisions they had with them. They had planned to only be away for a short period for this trip to the Temple, so they hadn't packed a great deal. He slipped his hand inside his bag, feeling the lumpy contents to check whether his memory served him well.

A pleasant smell wafted out as his fingertips brushed against some sprigs of rosemary, placed there to keep the contents of his satchel smelling fresh. There was a waterskin with a few sips left, and a beeswax candle, which left some waxy residue on his fingertips. A cloth parcel was filled with a handful of dried dates and some buttery biscuits, which were getting pulverized into fine crumbs as he handled them.

It was definitely not enough sustenance for what lay ahead. He would need to stop soon for some bread, a rind of cheese, and maybe some salty fish. He needed to stock up on provisions that wouldn't go rancid. Who knew how long he'd be traveling or where he would be able to obtain kosher food.

His fingers delved deeper into the bag and at last touched the most precious of his possessions, his beloved Torah scroll. Each day, he and his wife set aside time to learn the Torah, cherishing their moments of connecting with God. Sometimes the words stirred him, injecting him with energy and inspiration. Other times, they soothed his soul, calming his mood. Occasionally they left him uneasy as he tried to understand what the sentences meant, but they were always a welcome part of his routine.

After rinsing his hands with the remaining water in the skin, he unwrapped the thick cloth protecting the scroll. He unrolled it very slightly and ran his fingers over the smooth hide, tracing the black letters. The familiar characters brought some peace and comfort to his agitated spirit.

He was plagued with angst over the prophecy, but right now, it was the timing that really pained him. Practically speaking, of course, he was aware that it was only the sheer joy he had experienced in the Temple ceremony that had enabled him to receive prophecy. But the prophecy had tarnished one of his happiest moments—something he anticipated all year. It was common knowledge that those who had not experienced the events of the water-drawing ceremony had not seen true joy.

Even these days, when his hometown had little appreciation for the Temple, there remained a phrase from old times. It had all but lost its meaning, but it was considered the ultimate compliment and high praise to be offered after a wedding: "Finally, this one comes close to the joy of a water-drawing ceremony"—a *Simchat Beit HaShoeivah.*

Only, all of that had been marred. Now, the most joyous time of the year had a bitterness attached to it. The euphoria had been snatched from him, all for the sake of a wicked people undeserving of redemption.

Chapter 3

Tarshish

*a*s he packed away the Torah scroll, Jonah sensed his wife's presence. He looked up and saw that Shoshana had caught up to him. He owed her an explanation.

Her kind hazel eyes stared into his, full of confusion and bewilderment. She waited for him patiently. He barely knew where to begin, so it came out harsher than he had intended when he did speak.

"Go home!"

She looked at him like a startled doe, her eyes wide with fear.

"My dear Shoshana, I'm sorry." He breathed in deeply, nervously rubbing his worn, chapped hands together as he began again. "I received a prophecy during the *Simchat Beit HaShoeivah*. I have been charged with going to Nineveh to warn the people that their heinous ways have been noticed by God. They must repent or else be destroyed. It's too dangerous to take you on this journey and to expose you to such idolatrous and corrupt people. You need to go home."

Shoshana gasped. Her hands flew to her mouth in shock. "To Nineveh? But that is absurd…Why would God ask that of you? There is so much work to be done with the Israelite people; it doesn't make sense to go and help our enemy.

"And to what end?" his wife continued. "So they can heed your words and make us look bad? So they can live on to plan and plot against us?" The words gushed out of her like a fountain spurting water. "Oh, Jonah." She shook her head. "I'm so sorry you have to be the one to do this…"

"And what does this mean for us?" she asked plaintively as the realization hit her that they would be forced apart while Jonah was away on his mission.

He just looked back at her. He didn't have an answer, especially when he wasn't even planning on going to Nineveh. The only thing he was clear about was that he couldn't possibly drag her into all this. It was something he had to do alone. She would understand, he hoped. Her intuition was one of the traits he most admired in her.

"Who knows how long you'll be away." There was a catch in her voice, and her eyes welled up with tears of anguish. "I could come with you. I would undertake such a journey for God." She was no stranger to dangerous excursions. After all, though festival pilgrimage was optional for women, she had made this journey to the Temple, with all the risks involved.

"I must do this alone Shoshana. I cannot endanger you, nor do I want to burden you. We will stay together until just after we cross the checkpoint, but then we must say farewell."

She gazed at him quizzically. "Where are you going?"

He paused before replying. "To the Jaffa port," he said finally.

"Jaffa? But that doesn't make sense. You don't need a boat to get to Nineveh. You could travel by land..." Her voice trailed off as she understood the ramifications of what he was saying.

He wasn't heading to Nineveh.

Confident in his decision not to follow through with the word of God, Jonah realized he could go anywhere. It didn't take long to make a decision. Thinking through his options for a moment, his destination suddenly became obvious to him.

Inspired by the large, smooth turquoise stone hanging on the chain around his neck, he knew where he would go: Tarshish. He would travel to Jaffa, then he would catch a boat traveling northwest, toward Tarshish and far away from Nineveh.

It had to be Tarshish. Just pronouncing the name filled him with longing and desire. It was an ideal destination, a place that captured Jonah's interest and heart in so many ways. It reflected so much of his lineage and his dreams.

The stone hanging on the fine gold chain around Jonah's neck was a *tarshish* stone. It had been a gift from his parents. As a young boy, he had spent many long afternoons daydreaming about the location that shared a name with his stone—and was likely the place where the stone had originated.

Tarshish was a place of enormous wealth and riches, like those only found in fables and fairy tales. Only, this place was no legend; it actually existed. Somewhere, far away, there was a city called Tarshish, a land of gold, silver, and other precious metals and stones.

The High Priest in the Temple wore a gold breastplate fitted with twelve stones, each one representing one of the twelve Israelite tribes. This pale-green, aquamarine *tarshish* stone represented the tribe of Asher, his mother's tribe. Yet some Sages argued that it represented his paternal tribe of Zebulun. His parents had often lovingly reminded him of this debate. It was the very reason they had gifted it to Jonah, a son of both Asher and Zebulun.

Tarshish beckoned to him now as a fulfillment of his childhood dream. Some would suppose him seduced by the idea of escaping to a place of comfort, ease, and pleasure rather than the hardship and self-sacrifice that came with being a prophet.

But it was a different type of escape that tempted him. Tarshish was a secular city, godless. The knowledge of the one true God had not yet spread to Tarshish. This sparked his desire to flee there now and escape his current situation. He would rather be in a place without knowledge of God than a city like Nineveh, where they had rejected God and rebelled against Him.

Chapter 4

The Parting

They left Jerusalem. They had so much to say to each other and such limited time that neither of them ended up speaking.

Jonah didn't want to discuss his travel plans; he preferred to reflect on his dreams for their future. Their marriage had weathered many years of heartache and unanswered hopes. They had faced painful challenges as they waited and longed for children. He prayed that like the matriarchs and patriarchs, they would one day have a family.

He envisaged himself holding a young girl, a daughter, who would look just like his wife, with the same thick mass of dark curls and deep-set hazel eyes that took in every detail. Shoshana would be holding their baby, perhaps a little chubby-cheeked son, with dimples and a double chin, who would one day be a Torah scholar and take over the family mercantile business.

He opened his mouth several times to articulate these thoughts to his wife, then thought better of speaking of these desires. Instead, he shifted his attention to memories of himself as a youngster. He thought back to a childhood full of painful moments of waiting for his own father to return from his prophetic missions.

The quiet between Jonah and Shoshana became increasingly oppressive, heavy with all that needed to be said and with their fears for the upcoming events. Jonah found himself simultaneously frustrated and relieved by the silence.

Needing a distraction from his thoughts, Jonah mentally mapped out the route to Jaffa, the closest port to Jerusalem. He was tempted to go home first, to Gat Hefer, further north, close to the Sea of Galilee, in order to accompany Shoshana. He didn't like the idea of her traveling alone, but he was too anxious to get going. He couldn't afford the delay, nor could he prolong the inevitable. Before he departed, he would arrange for a reliable guide to accompany her home to at least ensure her safety.

They moved at a fast pace, picking up some supplies on the way. Before they knew it, they had reached the checkpoint.

He smelled the border long before he saw it, and a sense of dread filled him. It was the same every time, and it reeked of sweat, dampness, mold, and decay. It was the smell of his own fear, but it was also the smell of division and separation.

He hated that the border existed. One land, one people: that's the way it should be. This artificial divide, creating a rift in the Israelite people, made him so distressed. He longed for a reunion of the kingdoms, but he knew that it wasn't to be in the near future. There would be more tragedy and heartbreak to come before the land could be reunited.

It was always loosely guarded on the way into the Northern Kingdom—the guards less bothered about those entering the land than those leaving. Jonah and his wife crouched down low behind some bushes, taking advantage of the foliage dotting the open area.

A knot formed in Jonah's stomach. He and Shoshana muttered Psalms as they bided their time, watching and waiting for an opportunity to slip through.

The guards walked close by, paused to look around, then strolled back to the guard hut, taking a break from their sentry duty. Without hesitation, the two of them slipped past unnoticed and thanked God for a straightforward crossing.

They were now on the other side, cut off from the people in the Southern Kingdom and soon to be separated from each other.

Jonah stopped and turned to his wife, a woman of strength, conviction, and dignity. He took in the sight of her, trying to memorize every detail. This memory would have to keep him going for a while. He found himself drawn to her colorful headscarf, its ends waving in the wind as if bidding him farewell.

Her eyes were filled with tears that threatened to spill over. A few managed to escape, and those trickled down her cheeks in lonely paths.

Husband and wife gazed into each other's eyes. He uttered his goodbye and fervently murmured a prayer for protection and a safe journey for them both. Then, with great reluctance, he scribbled a divorce contract for her. It was painful to hand it over, but necessary.

She pushed it away, unwilling to accept this legal document that would mean the end of their marriage should he disappear, loath to accept this outcome to such a precious relationship. Nevertheless, he forced her to take it, to have the option in case he didn't return.

She tried to be strong for him. Her voice kept catching as she fought back the intense wave of emotion threatening to overtake her. "I would love to know what you're thinking, Jonah, or where you could possibly be heading. And who knows how God will respond to this...I just want you to come back to me in peace, please."

He nodded, admiring her for saying the right thing and putting God first, even in this most trying of circumstances. She would return to their house and maintain their business and routine, with or without him. He could rely on her. He withdrew and walked away from her. He turned back one final time to wave goodbye and saw her standing there, watching him, her arms wrapped around herself, her body shaking with grief.

With that painful image burned into his mind, he moved on.

He was so immersed in his thoughts about Shoshana and their home in Gat Hefer that his feet almost took him in that direction. He had to forcibly redirect his legs, reminding himself that he didn't have the time to detour. He needed to keep moving.

He walked by groups of merchants with laden donkeys, and some traders traveling by means of caravans of camels. It was the large and noisy family that captured his gaze, the mother flocked by a brood of small children.

Jonah spied some lemongrass growing on the side of the path, and he plucked some leaves to chew on to refresh his breath. He took the time to reflect on what his day would look like if he were already home.

Every time he and Shoshana returned from the pilgrimage, they would sit by the edge of the marketplace. Surrounded by people, mostly youngsters, they would share snippets of their awesome religious experience at the Temple.

He imagined himself there now, recounting the details of the water-drawing ceremony; reenacting the scenes of the priests drawing water from the Shiloah stream and pouring it onto the altar; narrating how he danced while singing songs and praises to God. In an effort to convey the lofty and joyous atmosphere in the Temple, he would throw the little ones up in the air and twirl them around. To end it off, there would be trumpet blasts, just as the priests had blown to indicate that morning had arrived.

Each year, Jonah tried to convince other villagers to join him and his wife on the triannual pilgrimage to the Temple. If the promise of being spiritually uplifted wasn't enough, he would try to lure them with the prospect of adventure.

He would regale them with tales of his bravery as he crossed the border between Judah and Israel just near Mount Baal-Hazor—stories detailing the flood of both fear and excitement that pumped through him in anticipation of the danger that lay ahead, or as he bribed guards to let him pass, or as he lay in wait, patiently seeking a gap in the border, disguising himself as a woodchopper or finding sympathetic guards to allow him through.

He would describe the tightness of his jaw—the result of steady fervent prayers muttered under his breath—and show them the way he would need to slow his breathing, inhaling and exhaling with long, exaggerated movements, in order to calm his body.

It was hard for the children to believe that the Temple was ever an attraction. The youth wore frowns of dismay and disbelief when he described the frequent visitors that had once flocked to the Temple from all over the land, especially for the three pilgrimage festivals. That there had been a time, before the split, when movement between the kingdoms had been free and unrestricted, seemed like fantasy to them.

Nowadays, there were very few travelers between Judah and Israel; the border was too heavily guarded. He spoke quietly when he narrated that part of history, not wanting to draw the attention or wrath of those in power. As a prophet, he was known to be contrary and outspoken, but inciting others was considered a step too far.

Sometimes, the adults would stand and listen too, pausing from their work as they gazed into the air, almost as if they could see the events unfolding before their eyes. More often than not, they would cluck their tongues at him and wag their fingers, convinced he was leading the children astray with his fanciful stories.

They insisted that there was no need to go to the Southern Kingdom of Judah, since they had all they needed right there in the Northern Kingdom of Israel. Who needed to make a pilgrimage to the city of Jerusalem, they would protest, when dazzling idols of golden calves and decadent temples were situated close by in Bethel and Dan?

It was a mentality Jonah couldn't even begin to understand, let alone tolerate. Jeroboam, the son of Nebat, the first king of the Northern Kingdom of Israel, had been all too successful in his scheme to draw the Israelites' attention away from Jerusalem in a bid to maintain his political power. Since then, other kings of the Northern Kingdom—Ahab the most notorious of them—had continued along this path, growing more powerful and strengthening the people's idolatrous ways.

This year, Shoshana alone would deliver the colorful account of their trip. He wondered whether she would forego it, waiting for his return so they could do it together. He should have discussed it with her, but with everything on his mind, silence had prevailed.

He cast his mind back to when they had first met, in the marketplace. She was youthful, with a constant smile etched on her face. There always seemed to be children around her—siblings, nieces, nephews—clinging to her or frolicking nearby. Whenever she looked up from her needlework and saw him watching her, she would blush, her entire face flushing a rosy red.

He searched for opportunities to speak to her, and excuses to buy some of her wares. He marveled at the deep colors she favored and how she skillfully wove them into stories. In her expert hands, the simple strands of thread became something much more than the sum of their parts. The rich cloths' seams and textures had called out to him. He briefly wondered what tales her threads would reveal now.

He missed her already. Her wit, the sound of her voice, her laughter, her wisdom and practicality, not to mention her cooking.

What wouldn't he give for one of Shoshana's baked goods right now?

He doubted they would keep well on a journey, but then he wouldn't know. They never lasted long enough in their home to cool down! As soon as Shoshana took those steaming flatbreads bursting with fresh herbs off the fire, he would polish them off.

Occasionally she would protest, ordering him to leave some for later. In light jest he would interrupt, exclaiming that God had made her an excellent cook so her food could bring him to a state of joy conducive to prophecy.

Memories flashed through his mind of his wife beaming with pride at his appreciation for her food. Her absence pained him, but he had a duty to carry out, a burden he needed to shoulder alone.

Chapter 5

The King

*a*s Jonah continued his journey, he couldn't help thinking back to his past prophecies—one in particular. It had left a bitter taste in his mouth.

It irked and infuriated him to hear that yet again he was being forced into a similar position. Once more, he was being asked to deliver good news to a wicked king. The last time had been to tell the Israelite King Jeroboam II, son of Jehoash, that the Northern Kingdom would experience military and financial gain, despite their wrongdoing. This time around, it was to give the wicked king of Nineveh the option to repent and save his city.

He could recall the event as if it had taken place yesterday. Just the thought of it was enough to induce physical symptoms. His heart started to pound furiously, and he felt shivers of terror course right through him. It hadn't been a pleasant experience standing before King Jeroboam II.

The entrance to the palace was lined with rows of soldiers, each one's gaze fixed straight ahead, barely blinking as Jonah walked past. Their uniforms were neat and freshly pressed, in shades of beige and brown. They grasped metal spears in their right hands which gleamed as though they had just been polished.

Their presence intimidated Jonah somewhat, but he was in such shock and fury over the other sights that he barely paid them any more attention than they seemed to be giving him. It was the assortment of statues and idols decorating the palace that made Jonah pause.

He passed imitations of animals and birds, trees and humans. Some were lifelike and full of detail, while others were simple, roughly hewn carvings. There were inked drawings alongside wooden, stone, clay, and ivory objects. The display made his blood boil. He averted his gaze upward and tried not to look at any of them as he hurriedly made his way through the palace.

The monarch's absolute power was visible in the splendor of his clothes, the extravagance of his jewels, and the way those clustered around him pandered to his needs, terrified to slight or upset him in any way.

The king sat in full regalia on an enormous and ornate throne. As much as Jonah fought it, he found his eyes constantly drawn to the king's lap. There, positioned on a plush purple pillow—a color reserved only for the monarchy—lay a bejeweled figurine of the fertility goddess, which the king was absentmindedly stroking. The offensive object, and the affection held for it, repulsed Jonah.

When Jonah opened his mouth, he wanted to let loose a torrent of abuse to rebuke and publicly berate the king for his spurious ways. He wanted to tear into Jeroboam's flesh like sharp arrows or a bird's talons. In his head, he was castigating the king for spreading idol worship and reinforcing social injustice among the Israelite people.

Instead, with an expression of indifference, Jonah stood there facing the king and delivered the positive news about the expansion of the Northern borders.

Some part of him was pleased with the prophecy, for he wanted only blessing and favor for his people; he loved and championed his nation. It was wonderful to bring them news of political stability and economic prosperity.

There was also the relief he felt when a prophecy had been delivered and his mission fulfilled. His struggle however, lay in delivering a favorable report to such a corrupt leader.

He remembered the pressure of his fingernails on the palms of his hands as he had clenched his fists in an attempt to maintain his composure. It was only when he left the palace and its debauchery behind that he opened his fists, revealing the deep indents made by his fingernails. That was the only physical sign of the inner turmoil he had faced while confronting the king.

The king had worn a smug smile throughout. With a sly gleam in his eyes, he had commanded his priests to organize a sacrifice in one of their temples as thanks to the God of Israel for this wonderful news. He ordered festivities and parties to celebrate that God was on their side. Sickened by Jeroboam's hypocrisy, Jonah could only comfort himself with the words of the prophet Amos that echoed in his head, knowing that one day soon the king would be punished.

That one time had been difficult enough for Jonah. At least then he had been able to console himself with the fact that the Israelite people had benefited. Now, once again, he was being sent to a wicked king with comforting news. The king, along with his people in Nineveh, were committing acts of violence, theft, and idolatry, among many other misdemeanors. Where they should be met with punishment, they were receiving a chance at atonement and forgiveness.

But this time it was much worse. Not only would these people have the opportunity to atone for their immoral ways, but it would be to the detriment of the Israelite people.

Jonah sped up as he tried to deal with the simmering rage and the swirling emotions inside him. For many years, prophets had urged the people of Israel to repent and change their deeds. They called on the people to stop social injustice, cease worshipping false gods, and return to the One true God and His ways.

His people, stubborn and obstinate in their lifestyle, wouldn't heed the prophets' words. But one day, Jonah was confident, the people of Israel would repent and reform. And when they did, their transformation would be a true and lasting metamorphosis. He suspected that Nineveh would listen to him and superficially reform their ways in order to avoid imminent punishment. But the contrast would be awful; the people of Israel would be painted in such a negative light. Jonah couldn't let that happen.

Moreover, Jonah had seen the possibilities of the future. He knew what could be. He had seen what the armies of Assyria could do to the Israelite people. His visions showed in great detail those cruel enemy soldiers flooding the Northern Kingdom of Israel. He saw the attack play out like a Game of Ur. First they would lay siege to the capital and then capture all of its inhabitants and exile the ten tribes, separating them from the land and scattering them all over the Assyrian empire so that they would be assimilated and lost forever.

There were times when it was a gift and a privilege to be a prophet, to share an intimate connection with God, to be a conduit and spread His word. However, moments like these were intensely painful and difficult. Foreseeing the possible tragedies and difficulties to come, and living through them alone, was a painful and deeply isolating experience. Vivid images of soldiers on horses, swords and spears, starving children, rivers of blood, and piles of corpses kept replaying in his mind. He composed himself and tried to clear his mind of those violent and bloody scenes.

Chapter 6

The Boat

Jonah was nearing the port of Jaffa now, some two days walk from Jerusalem. It was refreshing to be greeted with the fresh and salty smell of the sea. A wet breeze tickled his nostrils. Jonah stuck out his tongue to catch some moisture from the air and taste the saltiness. He inhaled deeply, allowing the scents to wash over him, attempting to ease some of the tension from his body.

The scent triggered recollections of himself as a young boy, frolicking on the shore, kicking and splashing in the waves. It conjured up fond childhood memories of visits to his maternal grandparents who had lived on the coastline.

It also brought to mind his recent experiences at the docks, haggling for goods, bargaining over prices, and patiently waiting for his valuable merchandise to arrive from destinations far and wide. Being in the Zebulun clan meant that he had been brought up learning the ins and outs of the business. As such, he felt very at ease at the noisy ports, where so much of their trade took place. In fact, the maritime industry was such an important part of their economy that the flag of Zebulun was a boat.

Seafaring wasn't just a convenient means of escape for Jonah; it held deep personal significance. It offered him familiarity; a piece of home comfort. Of course, he couldn't be faulted for hoping that the additional factors, such as the strong rocking motions of the boat and the poor company of loutish sailors—men of ill-repute—would be less-than-ideal conditions for prophecy.

JAFFA WAS BUSTLING. As the main port of Israel, it was teeming with action and brimming with people. Jonah was familiar with the sights from his frequent visits to Jaffa, but this time he tried to take it in as though with new eyes.

Being the successful merchant he was, the traders were the first people to catch his eye. Roaming the area, they were busy negotiating sales and overseeing the loading and unloading of their merchandise, as workers hauled crates across the dock to be transported by donkey or mule.

He noticed the vendors manning makeshift stalls where they were selling their wares, mainly cargo just off the boats. The fishermen strolled around with nets filled with their catch. Passengers hovered, easily recognizable as such by the luggage lying next to them or cradled safely in their arms.

Groups of sailors swarmed the port. There were the weary, sweaty, and grimy men relieved to have returned safely from their voyages and excited to have reached dry land. Then, not far from them, were the eager sailors bidding emotional farewells to their wives, trying to pry children off their legs as they prepared to embark.

A line of large ships was anchored near the shore. Some appeared more seaworthy than others. Many of them flew brightly colored flags indicating their point of origin.

Jonah hurried over to the vessels to inquire where they were heading, dodging piles of dung and refuse buzzing with flies as he went. Finally, after a handful of abrupt responses, he was rewarded with a helpful reply. A young, friendly sailor on an old and tired vessel with flaking paint and weathered wood informed him that he might be in luck. An unknown ship had been spotted making its way to Jaffa.

Jonah made his way through the throngs of people to wait for said ship. As he passed through the crowd, friends and fellow merchants shouted greetings to him. Some of the Israelites recognized him as a prophet. They moved aside, nodding their heads out of respect, smiling and acknowledging him. A few shoved their young children toward him, excited to be in the presence of the holy prophet, one or two even trying to grab onto his fur cloak. There were those with less pleasant things to say as well, but Jonah had grown used to ignoring them.

Standing at the edge of the rough timber platform, squinting out at the sea, Jonah could discern a ship in the distance. Much as he tried, he couldn't spot the flag. He tried to decipher the figurehead at the ship's bow to determine its origin; it appeared to be a carving of a peacock. It looked promising, as Tarshish was famous for its peacocks, but he was well aware that there was only a slim chance of the ship heading in that direction. Due to the long and arduous nature of the journey, ships to Tarshish were infrequent at the best of times.

He waited eagerly for it to draw closer, so full of excitement that he found himself bouncing on the soles of his feet. He was being overly optimistic. As the large, sturdy ship approached, it indeed appeared to be one of the magnificent Tarshish ships which were renowned for the skillful craftsmanship with which they were built. He waited, praying under his breath for it to be the one.

Peering intently, he could just about make out some of the facial features of the sailors onboard. He cupped his hands around his mouth and shouted in their direction to inquire where the ship was heading.

Those standing around him looked on with astonishment and curiosity, moving a few steps away to distance themselves from his eccentric behavior.

Then, from the boat, a few gruff voices shouted back some replies. It sounded vaguely like "Tarshish."

Could it really be? he wondered in surprise, or was he just hearing things, imagining the answer he was hoping for?

Then, one voice rang out as clearly as the peal of a bell, "Tarshish!"

Jonah's spirits soared. "Unbelievable," he murmured. Surely this was an auspicious sign that it was the path he was meant to take.

As soon as the ship neared the dock, preparing to moor, Jonah readied himself. He leaped aboard with incredible confidence and agility, not even waiting for them to anchor and dock.

There was a loud commotion from the shocked crowd gathered behind him. A number of the sailors exclaimed over his enthusiasm, eyeing him warily. They tossed lines to the dock workers who were ready, waiting to catch them and moor them to the large wooden posts.

"The captain," Jonah called out in Aramaic—so all could understand him—as he strode across the deck. "Where is the captain? I want to leave now."

The crew looked at each other, and their muttering grew louder, but Jonah ignored them in his haste to set sail.

A tall man with broad shoulders, a bald head, and a dark bushy beard stepped forward to greet Jonah and introduce himself. "I am the captain," he announced.

Jonah acknowledged him with a nod of his head. Then, in an assertive tone, he said, "Take me to Tarshish, please."

The captain responded coolly. "Apologies, my lord, but we are just returning from sea. Stormy weather forced us to cut short our voyage and return to port. We need to dock here and check the ship for damage, then replenish our supplies. Besides, the sailors have well earned a rest after their hard work navigating through the difficult conditions. A short spell on dry land with some wholesome stew or broth will aid their recovery. Not to mention some beer and ale to give them back their strength." He laughed.

The sailors chuckled along with him. Jonah could sense the camaraderie between the sailors; they seemed like a close-knit crew who respected their captain.

"No," answered Jonah. "We leave now. I will pay the fares for the entire ship, and for any other passengers you could have taken. I will pay before we even depart. Four thousand gold coins."

There was an audible gasp, followed swiftly by a hushed silence. If Jonah hadn't captured their attention before, he certainly had now. This was an offer that was difficult to refuse.

From inside his robe, Jonah drew out a large, bulging brown purse. He handed over the heavy pouch. The captain carefully weighed it in one hand, then proceeded to untie it and examine the contents.

It was filled to the brim with gold coins.

His eyes opened wide at the sight, his pupils dilating in delight. Selecting one coin at random, he brought it to his mouth to take a bite. He bit down hard on the coin, revealing a mouth with healthy pink gums and most of his teeth intact, though a large number of them were stained yellow and brown.

Satisfied that the gold was indeed genuine, he sent one of the sailors to fetch his scales so he could weigh the coins and confirm the amount.

Once weighed and counted, he secured the purse, pocketed it, and nodded toward Jonah with a look implying agreement.

Relieved and excited, Jonah settled himself and his satchel on the side of the deck so as not to bother the crew. He looked around, observing the group of sailors. It was made up of males of all ages and races, representing the seventy nations of the world.

They all shared some common physical features: large muscles formed by the physical exertion they engaged in daily, and lined, weathered faces, reflecting the quantity of time spent outdoors in harsh weather conditions.

As the ship set sail, he ignored the flurry of activity taking place and gazed into the distance. He had much to think about and was content looking out at the gentle, dark blue-gray waves of the surrounding sea.

He needed to focus on maintaining control of his body, as the force of the prophecy threatened to erupt from him with the power of a lion's roar. The vastness of the ocean brought him peace. Every so often, he would break his meditation to observe the movements of the crew rowing, their muscles bulging and shoulders rolling, or the quiet way in which the captain walked around, supervising and encouraging his men.

Accustomed to regularly appraising merchandise for his own trade, Jonah couldn't help casting long glances at the ship's cargo stacked close to him. He was certain that the bulk of it was stored below the deck, most likely under lock and key to prevent any pilfering.

The barrels and kegs piled near him were crafted from a type of dark wood that was unfamiliar to him. He was curious to know what tree produced this kind of wood. Just the workmanship of the barrels alone could certainly demand a high price in the market. Something like this would be ideal to recoup some of the sum he had just handed over. Four thousand gold coins was an absolute fortune; it would take him a long while to amass anything close to that in the near future.

He wasn't even sure what had prompted him to bring such a large sum with him on his travels. It would have been safer to leave it hidden at home rather than expose it to the risk of pickpockets and thieves. Now it was clear to him that it had been part of a Divine plan. It had been the right decision to bring it along, just as it had been to hand it over.

When he had placed it in the captain's hand, there had been a moment's hesitation and panic at the thought of handing over his fortune, but he had quickly overcome that difficulty. Once the gold had switched hands, he'd barely paid it a passing thought. Money was there to be used; it was a means, not an end. God had always been gracious to him; whatever he needed came through, and he was certain that would continue.

It had been a sunny morning when the voyage began, but now there were clouds overhead and a slight unseasonal drizzle. The air was moist but still warm, and despite the raindrops spattering on his head, Jonah was content to mentally review his Torah learning, the laws regarding the prohibition of idol worship. It seemed appropriate for his current situation, and the learning helped to calm his uptight body.

Sometime later, a number of the crew members started to take breaks. A few napped in their hammocks; others whiled away their time gambling, throwing dice, or playing fast-paced card games.

One sailor, a young bare-chested fellow, was giving haircuts with a sharp blade, shaving heads, and braiding long hair into complex weaves. A couple of older men exchanged stories, trying to outdo each other with their wild tales, liberally sprinkled with coarse cursing in various languages, all of which Jonah tried to shut out and ignore.

Chapter 7

The Storm

One sailor with a particularly thick accent chattered noisily to the crew member next to him.

"He's running from someone or something, I tell you. This ain't normal behavior. Maybe he's wanted by the king? Something ain't right here." As the sailor continued his monologue, his voice became more animated, rising in volume and reaching across the deck, even as far as the captain.

He continued, "You don't just jump straight on a ship and pay all that gold in advance; it's mighty suspicious. And where did he even get all that money from? He must have stolen it. I wager he's a thief or a swindler or…"

They never got to hear the rest of the accusation, as the man seated behind the speaker nudged him sharply in the ribs, interrupting the loud-mouthed man's flow. The captain was shooting him a stern glare. The sailor flushed bright red with shame, mumbled an apology, then turned his eyes downward and continued rowing in silence.

Jonah tried to keep his face blank and indifferent, pretending not to have overheard the outburst. He couldn't help the droll smile that crept to his mouth as he thought about how innocently he'd accrued his wealth—with Divine help, hard work, and by using the business acumen with which he had been blessed.

His running away wasn't so blameless, though. He may not have been a fugitive from the king, but he doubted an outlaw running from God was considered any better.

THE CAPTAIN SIGHED TO HIMSELF. He disapproved of his crew badmouthing passengers like that, but he agreed with what had been said.

After all, this impressive man, clearly of significant financial means, had sponsored the entire voyage in advance. Such an occurrence was unheard of. The fellow's impatience for them to set sail had been unusual too.

Then there was the extra something about this particular man. Some of the more superstitious crew members were calling it a godliness, and the captain was inclined to agree. Right from the start, he had stood out from the hustle and bustle of the crowd. Tall and willowy, this elegant and well-groomed man had a certain air about him.

The captain suspected this charisma had been a part of what had convinced him to acquiesce to the stranger's demands. Absorbed in the moment, he hadn't even thought to refuse him. Only afterward, once they had set sail again, had he remembered that the boat needed checking for repairs, provisions needed replacing and the restless crew could have done with a break.

Certainly, caught up in the excitement of the moment and with the enormous fortune of gold coins weighing down his hands, it had been hard to refuse the temptation. Yet if it was wealth he so desired, he could just run off with the valuable cargo the ship carried. Perhaps some sentimentality had crept through. Something about this man evoked positive feelings in him, reminding him of his eldest son, Jethro. It had been months since he had last seen his family in distant Tarshish, though only the gods knew that they occupied much of his thoughts. He hoped that someone was looking out for his Jethro.

COGNIZANT OF THE TENSE ATMOSPHERE and weary from his journey, Jonah decided it would be a good time to get some rest. He approached the captain to inquire about a place to sleep. With a warm grin, the captain offered to show him to his room.

As a cargo ship, they seldom transported passengers. On the rare occasion, the few passengers who joined the ship slept belowdecks on spare hammocks or straw mattresses. Movable panels could be set up as partitions to offer a modicum of privacy. However, a man of this passenger's standing deserved something better, so the captain was giving Jonah use of his own cabin.

Jonah followed the captain down the stairs, descending further and further into the bowels of the ship. With each downward step he took, he could feel his spirits plummeting and melancholy overtaking him. Finally, he was directed to the captain's cabin. With barely a glance at the large and richly furnished cabin, he threw himself onto the bunk to sleep. The straw mattress was sufficient, cushioning his body from the hard timber.

It could have been due to the clarity of mind that came with Jonah's heroic decision to run and protect the people of Israel no matter the cost—even to himself. Or perhaps it was an opportunity to remove himself from the world, a welcome distraction from his struggles with the Divine mission. Either way, ensconced in the cabin, slumber quickly embraced him.

A DAY INTO THEIR JOURNEY, seemingly out of nowhere, it looked like they were heading for a storm. What had begun as a straightforward navigation through calm waters with clear skies was becoming far more complicated. The waves turned choppy, the skies gray and overcast. They needed to pick up speed to move beyond the rough waters.

The captain urged his men to row faster, and told the second officer to adjust the sail to maximize speed. It was strange, because it wasn't the first bout of patchy weather they had faced.

Just four days earlier they had set sail from Jaffa. Then, two days into the voyage, they had hit such strong winds and stormy conditions that they had been forced to turn around and return to the port of Jaffa. If things had gone as initially planned, they would have been much further out at sea and would never have encountered their passenger.

As the weather became increasingly unpredictable, the sailors abandoned their games and stirred from their hammocks to focus on navigating the wild waters. A few hours later, the captain was very nervous. The storm showed no sign of abating; if anything, conditions were rapidly deteriorating. It made the storm they had faced a handful of days ago seem like child's play.

Winds were stirring up waves as high as the ship's mast. Sailors were bailing water out of the ship, using whatever was at hand, including kitchen vessels and utensils the cook was passing around. Others were busily tying down anything not fixed to the deck.

At least there was only one passenger to worry about, and he was safely stowed below deck, so they didn't have to spare him any attention.

The situation continued to deteriorate. The captain worked the ropes, trying to steer the ship on a different course, but it was a fruitless attempt. The tempest was too fierce. The heavy rain made it difficult to see ahead. Lashing winds and savage gusts whipped their faces. The boat's rocking motion was so violent and unpredictable that even seasoned sailors could feel their insides churning. The lucky ones managed to lean over the sides of the ship before losing the contents of their stomachs.

The sailors shouted to one another, growing more desperate and anxious. High waves sloshed over the sides of the boat, drenching them. A barrel that had been securely tied to the deck came loose; a rope uncoiled, and it was flung across the boat, winding its way around a sailor who was caught in its path.

The captain realized that they had no choice. The cargo would have to be tossed overboard.

Members of the crew rushed below the deck to bring up the cargo. With brute force, they smashed down the door, sending splinters of wood flying every which way. They herded the livestock up the stairs, accompanied by a loud cacophony of bleating and an unpleasant stench as the agitated animals loosened their bowels. Men hauled bales of textiles, sacks of flour, wooden crates, and earthenware jars across their backs, preparing to hurl them into the foaming waters.

They began throwing over anything they could see, with no care for what the containers held. A bag of grain split open as it was being heaved over the side of the boat, spilling a shower of tiny brown kernels into the water.

A sack of seeds ripped open. There was a strong sweet smell as some cloves tumbled out of a gash in another sack. One sailor tore open the supply of dried meat and passed it around for the men to chew, providing them with renewed energy and strength as they labored.

The captain didn't know which was worse: the loss of the supplies they required to survive the voyage or the precious and costly cargo.

All he could think was that only the gods knew what kind of priceless materials now lay at the bottom of the ocean.

The men threw the final item overboard—an empty cask that had once held aged red wine. It bobbed up and down in the water beside the ship. It was light and buoyant, and as the captain watched the barrel float, he couldn't help but think that it would make an ideal raft for some of the crew, if it came to that.

Sailors are a superstitious lot at the best of times—the inevitable consequence of dependence on the weather and sea. Each one had his own rituals and talismans and different gods on whom he relied. As the storm raged ferociously, the sailors muttered and prayed to their gods of the sea and storm.

One sailor made the mistake of loudly expressing sympathy for their passenger as he prayed, "Have mercy on the poor man who has chosen our ship."

Members of the crew turned on him in a fury, violently grabbing hold of his shoulders and shouting, "Pity him? It is his fault!"

They were quick to blame and curse the man they were transporting. As the sole passenger, with an unusual entry onto the ship, he made an easy scapegoat.

Chapter 8

The Lottery

a chain of sailors worked together, sweat dripping off their bodies as they attempted to bail the constant rush of incoming water out of the boat. There was little else for the captain or the rest of the crew to do besides examine their consciences and cry out to their gods for aid.

They had been praying fervently for a few hours already. Only one avenue remained: for the passenger to call out to his gods.

The captain hated to disturb their only passenger, but with the increasing ferocity of the wind and waves, it felt like the ship was being pulled apart at the seams. It was creaking and groaning under the strain of the storm. He had meant to have the boat checked over when they'd stopped in Jaffa—to see if it needed any tinkering or repairs—but unfortunately, due to the wealthy passenger's haste to set sail, that hadn't eventuated.

As the captain moved across the deck toward the staircase, the lookout ran into him, knocking him sideways.

With trepidation, the young pale-faced lad tried to speak, but his voice faltered. He mumbled a few words, but the captain was unable to understand a single one of them.

"Speak up, boy," boomed the captain.

The lad cleared his throat, and with some hesitation began to speak. "I can barely see anything through the haze and fog, but I noticed something strange. The storm is just around us."

Growing increasingly impatient, the captain quizzed him. "Be clear, boy. What do you mean 'just around us'?"

Other sailors flocked closer to hear the terse conversation.

"Captain," the lookout continued, "all around us the skies are angry and the waves are fighting with us, but beyond our ship all is calm. It's uncanny. It's as if the gods are telling us something."

As he finished speaking, the boy prostrated himself on the floor and began to passionately cry out to his gods. He gesticulated wildly, shouting out the names of all the gods he could remember.

The captain wished he could easily dismiss the claim as the product of a wild imagination, but he was feeling unsettled himself and had started to suspect that their run-in with the storm was the work of the gods.

He caught the eye of his second officer, a loyal and experienced sailor who had been with him from the beginning.

Braving the weather and struggling to remain upright, this sailor slowly made his way toward the mast. The crew held their breath, nervously watching him make the dangerous climb.

The captain received confirmation soon enough. On reaching the top, the second officer turned to the captain, with eyes full of fear, and nodded his head.

As the captain made his way belowdecks, his feet sloshing through the murky water that was pooling there, he couldn't imagine how scared their passenger must be. The ship was rocking so violently that he had to walk slowly and grasp onto the adjacent walls to keep himself upright.

It wasn't uncommon for passengers to become nauseous as they adjusted to sea travel. The captain presumed that he'd find the wealthy man sick and vomiting, huddled fearfully in the corner of his cabin. As he approached his lodgings, the captain knocked rapidly on the oak door, then pushed it open, calling out impatiently, "My lord."

To his utter shock and dismay, he found the man curled up on the bed, fast asleep. The forest-green blanket was tucked around him, almost covering his face, with just a hint of hair peeking through.

The captain stood and stared, his mouth agape. He was flabbergasted that the passenger could sleep when the life of every person onboard was at risk. The complacency of this man was such a contrast to the feverish pace with which his own men were working and praying to save themselves and the ship.

Suddenly enraged, the captain rushed over and shook the man awake, all niceties and servitude forgotten. Usually calm, he found himself shouting, spittle flying from his mouth as he yelled, "What are you doing sleeping? Arise! Call to your gods; maybe your gods will think of us and we won't perish."

Jonah stirred and opened his eyes to find the captain hovering over him, his face just inches away from his own. The captain, seeing him awake, seemed to come to his senses and took several steps backward, distancing himself from Jonah.

Jonah sat up calmly, shedding his blanket. He wrapped his cloak around himself, then turned to wash his hands from a cup lying in a basin near him. Surprisingly, the basin had retained some water despite the rocking of the boat. Quickly, he washed his hands and rubbed the sleep—and spittle—from his face. He followed the captain, who was moving up the stairs at a fast pace and turning his head every few steps as if to confirm that Jonah was following behind him.

While asleep, Jonah hadn't realized the predicament their boat was in. One didn't need to be a seasoned sea traveler to grasp the severity of the situation. They were struggling through a wild storm. Water was seeping through cracks, flooding the lower level of the ship.

He stumbled up the steps, plodding through puddles that soaked his feet with ice-cold water. The movement of the ship flung him around, and he knocked his head against the ceiling. Jonah braced himself on the narrow wooden beams next to the stairs. He didn't dare free a hand to rub the sore spot on his scalp; he needed both hands to grasp the supports in order to maintain his balance.

The words of the captain reverberated in his head. Surely it was no coincidence that he had echoed the very same words God had used to command him to go to Nineveh—"arise," and "call out."

The captain was in shock the whole way up the stairs. He kept glancing back at the voyager with incredulity. He couldn't comprehend the extent of his selfishness and passivity. The lives of his men were at stake as a catastrophic storm threatened to decimate them all, yet this man had been sleeping. No thought for the crew, the ship, or even himself.

The captain had been with the same ship ever since he had been appointed to the position, and losing this sturdy beauty would be as painful to him as losing a member of his crew. He shook his head in disbelief. No, the man hadn't spared a thought or prayer for any of them, nor did he seem to be praying now.

As soon as Jonah reached the deck, he was struck by salty blasts from the high waves lunging at them. It was foggy, with gusts of wind and rain. Those sailors who weren't busy trying to drain the water were hunched over and withdrawn, holding onto whatever was nailed down to the deck. They seemed relieved to see Jonah, as if they had been waiting for him to join them.

Immediately, a particularly muscular, burly figure with long, straggly black hair that was knotted from the furious winds stepped forward. He was cradling the ship's jar of stones in his arms, a means to conduct a lottery in this desperate hour.

The sailors surrounded him, huddling together. Using a small knife, the man carved a symbol representing Jonah onto a stone. He held it up for Jonah, the captain, and the crew to see, then dropped it into the jar. He muttered a prayer to an amulet hanging from a chain around his neck, then shook the container to mix the stones representing all those present on the ship. Placing his hand inside, he plucked out just one stone.

"The voyager!" he shouted.

The sailors turned to look at Jonah, and the thickset man handed the jar to a young man to the right of him. His pale face was tense and overshadowed with worry. With nails bitten and ragged from his nervousness, he picked out a stone. "The voyager," he declared.

His eyes wide, he passed the jar to the sailor next to him so they could again draw lots. Once more, the same stone was selected. Aghast, that sailor forced the jar into the hands of his neighbor. It couldn't be a coincidence that each time the same name was being chosen.

With trepidation, the next sailor let his long, spindly fingers take their time selecting a stone. As his choice was revealed, he gasped aloud. It was obvious which name had been selected—there was no need to call it out again.

All attention was now on Jonah. The lots had been drawn, the gods had spoken. Clearly this traveler was the cause of the storm and their trouble. The stocky figure who had been the first to pick out Jonah's name turned to him and, in a gruff voice, demanded answers. "Tell us, now, what is the cause of this evil that is happening to us? What is your job? Where are you from? What is your land? Who are your people?"

So many answers ran through Jonah's mind in reply to this battery of questions. Ignoring the fierce wind and icy spray, he thought about his response. *Should I tell them that I am a prophet? Should I disclose my name? Or my nickname?*

With great fondness, Jonah recalled his teacher, a kind and patient old man with soft and curly hair the color of fresh snow, who had awarded him his nickname. From a very young age, Jonah had been truthful, principled, and exact. Finally, after one too many clashes with his peers over sticking to his principles, the teacher had called him "Emet." It was a play on his father's name, Amitai, hinting at the Hebrew word *emet*, meaning "truth."

With a cool demeanor, Jonah answered succinctly, "I am an *Ivri*, a Hebrew, and I fear the Lord, God of heaven, Who made both the sea and the dry land." He paused, then added, "I am running from the presence of God and His Divine message to me. I am avoiding delivering His word to the people of Nineveh."

He felt a sense of pride in his identity. Here he was, a man of God, with a whole boatload of idolaters. Who knew what these boorish sailors might do to him or how they might react to his admission? However, as was his way, he would stick to the truth come what may.

He particularly relished his use of the word *ivri*. This one small word not only identified his people, it also managed to sum up so many of the conflicting emotions he was dealing with.

Ivri, a term implying wrongdoing, from the Hebrew word *aveirah*. He could see the sailors' faces. He heard their whispers. They were astounded and appalled that he could even consider running away from God and the gift of prophecy.

Ivri has another meaning too. It means "from the other side," and he was definitely feeling like an alien right now as they gaped at him.

Of course, they stared at him. The entire crew crowded around him, wide-eyed, with mouths open in shock and amazement. Jonah had just delivered a life-changing revelation. After a lifetime of worshipping various gods, visiting their temples, setting up altars, placating their priests and priestesses, and caring for their idols, they were hearing about a one true God. They were in the presence of a holy man, a representative of the Almighty, a trusted messenger who communicated with Him.

Monotheism was a foreign and novel concept to the sailors. The notion of one God in charge of everything—a potent God Who knew what was happening everywhere, so that one could sin on land and be punished at sea—blew their minds. Moreover, the idea that this powerful Presence could affect the life of just one man, and could control and direct the fate of just one ship—the concept hit them like a thunderbolt, shattering the facade they had lived with until that point.

The truth resonated with them.

Chapter 9

Overboard

*a*s Jonah finished speaking, the sea and storm grew wilder and more turbulent, as if in response to his words. As icy drops pelted them, the sailors, reminded of the urgency of the situation, bombarded him with questions and requests. Their unfamiliar foreign accents made it difficult for Jonah to understand what they were saying, especially with the loud whistling and howling of the wind.

They seemed to be asking him two things: "What have you done?" and "What do we need to do in order to calm the sea?"

What had he done? He was tempted to point out their shortcomings and blame the storm on these idolaters—rough, uncouth men with coarse language and loose morals could surely be faulted. But no, the storm was his fault and his responsibility. It was solely his doing.

"I am a prophet. I am running away from the Almighty, from Whom no one can run," he repeated. He saw several of the men exchange glances as he spoke.

Of course, he thought to himself, *I'm not trying to escape God Himself; it is impossible to evade He Who is Omniscient and Omnipresent.* Rather, Jonah was avoiding his mission. He couldn't bear to face Nineveh and bring the people to a state of repentance. He couldn't deal with saving a nation that would turn around and attack the people of Israel in the future.

And as far as what could they do? *Easy,* he thought, and then said aloud, "Throw me into the sea, and the waters will calm down." He had already decided that death would be his best option. He would rather die than cause harm to the Israelites.

The sailors reacted to Jonah's instruction with looks of shock and dismay. It seemed like the option hadn't even occurred to them. The idea of throwing a passenger overboard—let alone a man of God like Jonah—was preposterous to them.

Outraged, they ran to their recently abandoned positions at the oars and tried to row to land. It was hazy, raining, and hailing. There was no way anyone could spot land in these harsh conditions, but they would try. Once there, they could deposit Jonah and be done with the whole thing.

It was of no use, though. As much as they tried to change course, turn back, and head for dry land, they couldn't. All their efforts were in vain. The waves seemed to rise in opposition, challenging them, forcing them to give up. The sailors were weary and exhausted. The hours of work trying to save the ship had taken their toll. Additionally, the realization of what they had to do cast a heavy emotional and mental burden on them. Despite knowing that throwing their passenger overboard could save the ship and their own lives, the sailors were still reluctant to carry out the unspeakable act.

The sailors called out to the God of Jonah, now their God, for there was no question of His might and awesomeness after the events they had witnessed. The appearance and arrival of this unusual figure, the savage storm that had wreaked havoc on their ship, the lots that had directed them to their passenger, and, finally, his revelation, all confirmed their belief in one God Who ruled everything—both the dry land and the sea.

Tens of voices called out in various languages and dialects, requesting that God look after them and not let them die. One sailor took out a letter from his wife and pressed it close to his heart, kissing it before replacing it in a fold in his clothes. Some wept.

One man, who had only recently become a father, started bawling like a baby himself at the prospect of leaving his young wife a widow. Another, a bald sailor, kept running his hand over his smooth scalp, seemingly drawing comfort from this repetitive motion. Others were somber and grim-faced, with pursed lips and drawn brows, clearly apprehensive and terrified about what lay ahead.

"Don't hold us accountable," murmured one voice.

Another took up this line and shouted, "Don't blame us for his death."

Other voices broke through the tense silence with similar cries and chants to God. The atmosphere was thick and heavy with fear, guilt, and tension.

Only Jonah stood there seemingly relaxed and indifferent. His body did not betray him by revealing any sign of his internal battle. He stood looking out at the expanse of the sea. From a young age he had always found the open waters reassuring and comforting. The sight and sound of water had always implied possibility and adventure. It was ripe with options, full of promise. But now, the water's usual calming effect wasn't working its magic. The fierce storm only seemed to further stir the storm raging within him.

Having given his men a few moments to pray and collect themselves, the captain urged those closest to Jonah to grab hold of him.

Jonah didn't resist, but he didn't help them either. Like a rag doll, he allowed them to do with him as they wished. They wrapped a length of rope around his waist, knotting it securely. They then prepared to throw him overboard.

Reluctantly, they lowered the rope, until his toes dipped into the raging waters. The water was cold, and his sandals were torn off almost immediately, spiraling away into the current.

They lowered him further. The waters reached his knees. It made him think back to the *Simchat Beit Hashoeivah*. He wished he were back there now, knocking knees with the Israelite men as they danced and celebrated together.

Miraculously, the storm abated, and the sea calmed. Naked relief was evident on the sailors' faces as they gleefully plucked Jonah out of the water. But the waters immediately returned to their previous heights. Jonah heard the groans they emitted as their idea failed. Now, they lowered more of his body into the frigid water, until his navel.

Again the storm stilled. The waves pummeled his stomach, and he groaned in pain.

He was reminded of a time he'd been in the marketplace when a young boy collapsed, clutching his stomach and writhing in pain. A quick-thinking elder had scooped him up to take him for medical aid, and sent some youngsters to let his family know the situation. Unfortunately, the lad didn't make it.

It was a tragic loss, eased only by the wonder of seeing how the community rallied to comfort the family for months afterward. The kindness and care they had shown and the help they had offered had left a deep impression on Jonah. This was what he loved about the people of Israel. His affection for his nation was one of the main reasons he couldn't go to Nineveh.

This time, they pulled him out of the water with hesitation. It was harder to haul him out now; his robes were sodden and heavy. As they tugged on the rope, two more men had to come forward and yank under his arms to lift him over the side of the boat. Jonah wanted them to relinquish their hold on him, but he let them go ahead, content to be passive.

Once again, as Jonah had expected, the sea resumed its furious pace as soon as his feet had left the water. The waters were splashing upward, almost like arms trying to grab Jonah, reaching to pull him into their grasp.

With great reluctance, the men lowered Jonah once again. As his freezing toes entered the foam, the waters surrounding the boat calmed, just like the surrounding sea. This time, the sailors lowered Jonah down to his neck. He was shivering as the water covered most of his body. His shaking became uncontrollable as the pressure on his neck brought to mind the way the cruel Assyrians dealt with their enemies, beheading them. The heads were impaled on pikes and exhibited for all to see on the city's ramparts. Thoughts of the brutality of this people strengthened his resolve to protect the Israelite people at all costs.

The sailors were leaning over the side of the ship from the strain of supporting Jonah's weight, their muscles tiring as they struggled not to drop him into the iron-gray sea. Other sailors grabbed hold of the ones carrying him, forming a human chain to keep them safely anchored inside the boat.

Jonah felt himself being raised again. As his feet left the water and he was suspended in midair, he stared up at the sailors. Their faces were fearful. He willed himself to look into their eyes as it happened. As his intense gaze met theirs, it seemed to give them the permission they sought, and just like that, they released the rope and let him go.

Jonah fell into the water. As he descended, he watched the expression on the captain's face relax as the boat settled on the now calm waters.

It wasn't just morbid curiosity that had the sailors peering over the edge of the ship. They crowded the starboard side, vying to catch a final glimpse of their voyager, hoping for a sense of closure. Even knowing that Jonah was the cause of their problems, it had been difficult to throw him overboard; they felt pangs of regret and guilt at throwing a man to his death. Alongside the grief and mourning, there was also an immediate sense of relief that the saga was over. Some tears were shed for his loss, others cried for joy that their own lives had been spared.

Chapter 10

The Sailors

Jonah spluttered as his nose and mouth plunged underwater and he swallowed some of the murkiness.

He had thought he would embrace this end to his life. In his mind, it was going to be a relief and consolation, some kind of beautiful restorative process. He had imagined that, just like dipping in the waters of the mikveh, the ritual bath, this would provide him with spiritual and mental peace, a chance to wash away the negativity of the past few days and immerse himself in the water's loving envelopment.

The reality was a stark contrast. He coughed and retched as he was dragged under, his arms and legs flailing in desperation. He couldn't see the boat anymore; he couldn't even determine the direction of the surface. He was surrounded by blackness. The layers of his clothes and the weight of the rope dragged him deeper underwater. He started to panic as his oxygen supply depleted and water rushed into his nostrils, racing down his throat.

The darkness felt heavy, clawing and pulling at him. He felt clammy seaweed brush past him. Thin, long strands of seaweed wrapped around his torso, catching on his ankle, and then tightened like a lasso around his neck. He struggled to loosen the choking grip around his throat as the plant and water worked in tandem to asphyxiate him. Now that he was facing his demise, it was too much. His only relief was the thought that death was better than wronging the Israelite people.

THE CAPTAIN OF THE SHIP peered into the swirling waves long after the last sighting of Jonah's clothing. Mere seconds after he had been thrown overboard, Jonah had vanished.

There had been a moment of excitement when one of his sandals had surfaced. There was a collective intake of breath as the sailors watched, hoping Jonah would reappear. After a long wait, it became increasingly obvious that it was just a lone item of clothing, not attached to a body. Even that soon disappeared, sucked underwater again.

There was no trace of their passenger, and his body would probably never be found. Perhaps he was lying among the spilled treasures at the bottom of the ocean, surrounded by gold and jewels from Tarshish.

The captain allowed himself and the sailors some time to mourn and process what had just taken place. In the wake of these events, his crew was physically exhausted. Despite their fatigue, however, there was no time to rest. Bereft of provisions, the sailors were now in dire need of supplies and had to dock as soon as possible.

Fortunately, they felt inspired by their encounter with the man of God and the transformation he had brought. They were eager to reach dry land not just to eat, but in order to fulfill their vows to bring dedications to the poor and offer animal sacrifices to the God of Jonah.

There was worry that the unfavorable winds had pushed them off course. Disoriented, it took the sailors some time to study the maps and calculate their position. The lookout stood surveying their surroundings, gazing at the vast expanse of the sea. When he squinted his eyes, he could just make out a patch of dry land in the distance. They would head that way, hopefully making it in good time.

Sometime later there was a sharp cry from the lookout. "Land ahead!" He began yelling and jumping with enthusiasm. "We made it to Tarshish!" The glee was evident in his voice.

Sounds of shock and wonder filled the air. It was unbelievable that somehow they had made it to Tarshish. Hearing their destination, the crew rowed with more enthusiasm.

Though these seamen loved the ocean, the salty spray, the physical labor, and the camaraderie born of months at sea together, dry land held an appeal of its own. Right now, the sailors longed for firm, solid ground beneath their feet. They needed to repair and restock the ship and catch up on some sleep. They had earned a break and were eager to frequent the taverns, sate their hunger, and fulfill their vows to God.

THE SAILORS DISEMBARKED and merrily made their way to a small, popular tavern, well known for its tasty and homemade food. They walked together, a group of men, more like brothers than colleagues. The transformative experience had forged a deep connection between them, the type created only between those who had faced death and trauma together.

The strenuous exercise of rowing and steering a boat, not to mention the mental exertion and worry in which they had engaged, encouraged a hearty appetite. Ship fare was mostly dry goods like stale biscuits and crackers, often sampled by rats before it even reached the crew. It was less than appetizing, and sorely lacking texture and taste after prolonged exposure to the damp conditions onboard.

Even that plain fare, though, would have been welcomed by these sailors, who hadn't eaten since having thrown their supplies overboard during the storm. They were salivating at the thought of some food. They were fantasizing about the taste of some crusty bread and thick, hot soup.

The cook saw them approaching and recognized that these were men with great hunger and full purses. He, his matronly wife, and their three children, who helped prepare and serve the food in this establishment, were quick to take advantage of the situation. They hurried to attend to the men, bringing flagons filled with wine, rum, and mead, accompanied by bread straight from the oven, while taking their orders. The sailors dived in greedily and took solace in the fresh and tasty provisions. With full bellies, they were finally able to unwind and relax.

THE ALCOHOL SOON LOOSENED THEIR TONGUES, and they sat back, ready to tell the fantastic story of the man of God who had sailed on the boat with them. They described the mysterious and distinguished gentleman. Gasps and exclamations were heard as they relayed how he had handed over the entire ship's fare before the trip had even begun.

The locals and other seamen drinking in the tavern listened in rapture to their tale of the choppy waters and terrible weather conditions that had endangered the lives of all the sailors. A few of the sailors present in the tavern had actually witnessed a stretch of sea that seemed murky and stormy, even while the rest of the waters were tranquil. None of their boats had been affected; they hadn't even spotted a boat sailing in that dark patch, but they conjectured that it was possible. This affirmation seemed to lend enough validity to the story for those present and listening.

Their audience was shocked to hear that the voyager had slept throughout the tumult, and astonished to learn that the Hebrew's name was cast from the lottery every single time. As they reached the climax of the story, there was utter silence in the room. All those present were spellbound, and they hung on to every word. On more than one occasion, individuals looked in the captain's direction for a nod of verification. Sailors were known to spin tales; they needed amusement and distraction on their travels. But it was indeed rare for a captain to partake in such prattle.

As the sailors finished off the story with a description of dropping Jonah's body overboard, there were a few tears in people's eyes. Sighs escaped their lips. "What a tragic end," they exclaimed, "but at least, thank the gods, these sailors and their boat survived the calamity."

A few people struck up a conversation about this Almighty God to whom the sailors had vowed to pray and offer sacrifices. There was some speculation as to why Nineveh was deserving of this God's wrath.

The sailors left the tavern with full stomachs and heavy heads. They slept well that night, glad to be on flat and dry land, barely cognizant of how many of them were crowded in the barn and the sparse number of blankets available. Alcohol fumes and heavy snoring filled the air.

The locals, however, departed on a high, bursting with excitement about the strange and wondrous tale they had been told. Too animated to sleep, they were eager to return home and share the fascinating tale of the night with their families and neighbors.

THE CAPTAIN HAD EXPECTED the news to travel, but it happened faster than he had predicted.

Midmorning, the sailors were woken by the noisy arrival of a group of officials. The disgruntled sailors emitted loud mumbling and grumbling, until they realized that these officials were tax collectors.

The captain rose and dressed in haste, hurrying into the tavern to meet with them. The officials demanded an explanation for the whereabouts of the valuable cargo; its absence meant a huge financial loss for them. In a secluded area they sat and listened in disbelief to his account of the events that had taken place over the last few days.

They interviewed the sailors one by one, hurling accusations of theft at each one of them and challenging them on minor details to confirm that their stories tallied up. When the officials finally accepted their reports as the truth, they wanted to immediately send word to Nineveh—the destination avoided by the man of God. After all, if his God could storm the sea, then He could also wreak havoc upon land. Nineveh was the capital of the powerful Assyria; it could only serve in their best interest to provide a warning. They were hoping for a financial honorarium that would mitigate their recent monetary losses.

It was decided that the officials would accompany a few of the sailors on the trip to Nineveh to deliver the news to the king and personally testify about the threat of this God.

They planned to leave the following day and travel until they reached the River Tigris, then take the quppu ferry along the network of canals into the city. They hoped to avoid the heavy rainfall of the early winter. A handful of sailors volunteered for this mission, lured by the prospect of adventure and prestige, one or two of them also contemplating leaving a life at sea and remaining in Nineveh.

Chapter 11

The Fish

a strange sensation overcame Jonah's body as he was brutally tossed around by the waves. It felt like he was being squeezed between red-hot pincers. A vice-like grip seemed to clamp down on his ribs, crushing him.

Then, abruptly, just as he felt he was at his breaking point, his whole body slipped downward in a free fall. The loss of gravity was terrifying, and he felt his stomach drop. He opened his mouth to cry out, but he was too terrified to make a sound. Instead, a silent scream escaped.

His body slammed down hard, left shoulder first, onto a wet surface. Immediately, he was enveloped in an acid-like substance that penetrated the outer layer of his skin. The thick, gooey slime covered his clothes and body, making it tingle and sting as if he were aflame.

Waves of nausea washed over him. Instinctively, he inhaled, greedily sucking in the available oxygen. His breaths triggered a violent coughing fit, and his body struggled to expel the water from his lungs. He lay there coughing and spluttering. His chest ached, and his throat felt raw. Every breath he took was painful, but he welcomed the feeling of being alive.

Unfortunately, his relief was short-lived. The barrage of attacks on his body had left him beaten and battered, and he was in terrible agony. He had nearly drowned. His fingers automatically clutched his nostrils as he recalled how the water had pushed and swelled against them, creating such intense pressure.

Now, in addition to all the pain he'd already been subjected to, his body was being scalded.

He emitted moans and wails at this new form of torture.

JONAH LAY CURLED UP IN A FETAL POSITION, his figure limp and bruised. Once more, he felt ready for death.

It was pitch black; he couldn't even see his fingers when he waved them in front of his face. He recoiled in disgust at the sounds of legs scuttling about and things slithering around. He felt a prickling sensation, as though small insects were crawling all over his body. He repeatedly flicked and swatted at his limbs in an attempt to remove them, although he was uncertain whether the sensations were real or imagined.

There was a sloshing noise around him as the shallow pool of acidic liquid splashed and splattered. His side was raw from lying in this fluid. He tried to use the tatty remains of the rope and his cloak to shield his body from more pain.

The stench was so terrible, he couldn't help but retch. Over and over again he heaved, whimpering as his empty stomach knotted and twisted like damp clothes wrung out by a washer woman. He had last eaten on the journey to Jaffa...When had that been? His violent stomach cramps made it difficult for him to think clearly.

In the midst of his pain, he suddenly came to the realization that he was inside the stomach of a large fish. Was such a thing even possible? Oh, how greatly he questioned his mental state. Was he perhaps losing his sanity?

It occurred to him that he could be dead. Maybe he had actually drowned and was now in the afterlife? The whole notion of being inside a fish was so peculiar and outlandish, yet it was also the only thing that made sense.

In light of this epiphany, Jonah found it very hard to maintain a sense of calm and well-being. His breathing sped up, and he was close to hyperventilating.

A sudden noise shocked him. It sounded like there was someone with him. He moved his head to listen better, before realizing that he was hearing his own nervous giggles. The chortles soon turned to howls, which became deep, racking cries and wails.

In sudden panic, he clawed at his upper chest, feeling around for his necklace. It was one of the few things he owned that he really cared about. It was irreplaceable. His bag and provisions were gone; only God knew where they were. He slumped in relief when his fingers met the smooth stone.

He realized, belatedly, that his beloved Torah scroll was lost too. A fresh wave of pain washed over him. Oh, the anguish of being separated from his wife—and now his Torah. It was another beating to his already broken heart. Sobbing, he rocked to and fro, his hands clutching the cool stone tightly as though begging it to comfort him. At least he still had his necklace.

He was suffering, but he tried to focus on the positive aspects of his situation: This fish was his savior. It had swallowed him in the nick of time. And now it was protecting him and housing him, allowing him to live. Despite acknowledging all these benefits, he couldn't help but question why, if God were going to send him a champion, did it have to be such an unpleasant experience? Was he being ungrateful for this sanctuary?

As Jonah contemplated his situation, he noticed a recurring theme of escape in all his recent struggles: leaving his wife, fleeing the land of Israel, being thrown off the ship, trying to escape from this world, and now his desire to leave the fish. Maybe it was time to stop running away. Every time he ran, God was there, both to comfort and confront him.

Generally speaking, before receiving this prophecy Jonah hadn't been the type of person who ran away from troubles and problems. He considered himself a responsible and committed individual—solid and dependable. He never physically withdrew from his problems, never tried to escape from accounts to be paid or issues to be resolved. He'd always been able to handle whatever came his way. What was happening to him now?

The hunger, pain, and solitude were making him agitated and disoriented. Here he was, confined, alone in this thick darkness, deep in the depths of the sea. Visions of food clouded his mind.

Half delirious, he began to mumble. "We remember the fish we ate in Egypt for free," he quoted from the Torah, from chapter eleven of Numbers. It was a passage about the fish the Israelites had craved in the desert as did he now. The Israelites—himself, then—now...it all seemed to merge into thoughts of hunger and eating fish.

Hadn't they realized that they had a land gifted to them by God, that they had no right to mourn their life of slavery in Egypt? They were missing what God wanted from him.

Not him. He meant *them*. *They* were missing God's intention. His mind was confused.

Don't you realize, a voice mocked him, *that you too are chasing the fish of your idyllic fantasy rather than facing the hard reality of where God wants you to go?*

As the plot grew ever more insane, the rocky movements of the fish seemed to slow and relax. At a certain point—Jonah wasn't sure exactly when—he realized that the fish's movements had become steadier, and it was easier for him to maintain his balance and position. What had begun as a voyage of frantic rocking and swooping had slowed to a gentle bobbing.

The dulled motion was a welcome blessing, until Jonah understood the reason for it—the fish was dead. Unfortunately, with the calm came an ever-worsening smell of rotting flesh and decay.

It was a stark reminder of his own mortality—not just because he was encapsulated by death. Rather, it was the realization that the fish carcass was all that separated and protected Jonah from his own demise.

Issues of life and death and second chances occupied his thoughts. How could they not, when they reflected so much of his past? His father, also a prophet, had died when Jonah was young. That had been a painful and difficult period for him. His mother, a strong-willed woman, had brought him up alone, a single mother doing her best to provide for her only child.

He had vivid memories of her kneading dough with her deft fingers, flour flying through the air as she worked, leaving smudges on her cheeks that highlighted her hollow cheekbones. Whenever her eyes, a deep brown like roasted nuts, caught sight of Jonah, a broad grin would illuminate her face.

Then there was the serendipitous encounter that had changed their lives. The great and famous prophet Elijah, fleeing from King Ahab and Queen Jezebel, had approached his mother, requesting her assistance.

The three experienced the daily miracle of having enough flour and oil to feed them. Unfortunately, even that wasn't enough. A year later, Jonah had almost died due to the terrible famine conditions.

Elijah had been lodging with them, and he stepped in to perform a miracle, bringing Jonah back to life. Jonah's life was never the same after that. That intimate life-saving moment transformed their relationship. Like a father, Elijah had given him life, and Jonah became like a son to him.

He looked up to and admired this father figure, a substitute for his own. He tried to emulate him in every way possible, and as a youth, would often copy his form of dress, taking careful note of the colors he wore and the way he tied his headwear. His own mantle, a cloak of fur, was just like the one Elijah wore. He regularly studied with him, and adopted many of Elijah's attributes, such as his fierce commitment to the truth and staunch loyalty to God. Jonah felt an equally strong love and devotion toward God, but as the "child" of Elijah, he felt it more fitting that his zeal was directed toward God's child, the Israelite nation.

His near-death experience at sea brought both the passing of his father and his own previous encounter with death to the forefront of his mind. These brushes with mortality made him feel dispirited and dejected. Elijah would have understood this as well; he too had suffered bouts of self-doubt.

Jonah's spirits were low, like the physical lows he had occupied in the ship, in the ocean, and now in the fish. Having first been physically dragged down by the ocean current and seaweed, he was now being pulled down by his melancholy. He was broken and vulnerable.

He couldn't stay in the fish any longer. More to the point, he refused to die in the fish. It had taken almost dying for him to realize that he didn't want to die. He wasn't prepared for the finality of death. He knew he would miss Shoshana and mourn his people, but, more than that, the thought of never seeing the Temple again was most distressing for him. The precious Temple was the place where this mission had begun. It was there that he'd shared an intimate relationship with God, experienced true joy, mingled with his brethren, and received prophecy.

IT WAS THIS LONGING FOR LIFE that persuaded Jonah to call out to God. Finally, after three days of suffering in near silence, Jonah was ready to talk. He was desperately lonely and craving connection. In general, he enjoyed his own company, reading or learning alone in the early hours of the morning or late at night.

This, however, felt different. This was a forced encounter with himself in the pitch black, under claustrophobic conditions, all while suffering from pain, hunger, and the horrible odors of rot and decay.

Jonah cried out to God. "You cast me into the depths, into the hearts of the sea. The floods surrounded me, all your waves swept over me."

Even at this lowest point, after running away from the Divine will, Jonah knew that he could still turn to God, and he would never be turned away. As he began to open up and speak to God, he became increasingly confident that He would save him. After all, why go to the trouble of arranging a fish to rescue him from death if the Almighty didn't intend to release him?

As a thanksgiving for the coming rescue, he promised God that he would offer sacrifices. He presumed that the sailors had pledged to do the same. Until now, he had barely spared them a thought, but now that he thought about it, they hadn't been as ill-mannered and wildly behaved as he had expected.

Still, though, he was certain they would have made all sorts of desperate promises to God, anything to deliver them from the turbulent storm.

He continued his prayer. "Those who worship false gods have lost their source of mercy. But me, I will offer a sacrifice to you with a voice of thanks. That which I have promised, I will fulfill."

Those fair-weather friends would look to God and commit to Him when times were tough, and they were in need. Then, when life improved and the wild seas calmed down, they would quickly forget about the whole experience, including their promises to God. All their pledges—gifts for the poor, animal sacrifices, maybe even circumcision and conversion—would all be dismissed once they were saved.

In all these thoughts, it didn't occur to Jonah that his own prayers had been prompted by the abject distress he was enduring in the fish. He was guilty of the very thing of which he was accusing the sailors.

Chapter 12

A Second Time

*a*s his prayer drew to an end, the fish suddenly came to life. Before Jonah could even process what was happening, the fish had swooped upward and ejected Jonah, violently casting him out of its mouth onto the shore. The giant fish, having completed its duty, disappeared into the water, sucked beneath the surface without a trace.

Seamen and dock workers laboring nearby saw the event unfold. They stood around watching in disbelief.

Jonah had been tossed onto the sand like a piece of refuse. He'd been knocked unconscious when he landed, and it was in that state that he once again received a prophecy. The voice of God filled him, commanding him to go to Nineveh.

When he awoke, he lay motionless in a state of shock and weakness. It was only after he'd ventured to test that his limbs were still in order and stretched his neck to survey his surroundings that it became obvious to those watching that he was, in fact, alive.

Jonah looked a fright. He was covered in mucus and slime, and his skin was red and peeling. The forcible regurgitation had caused his fragile skin, already burned and injured, to pain him anew. His left shoulder, damaged during his descent into the fish, was bruised and throbbing.

He tried to speak up and ask those around him where he was. His throat was so parched and sore that it took several attempts before he could faintly rasp the question.

Not hearing him clearly, a few brave men drew closer until his voice was audible. No one else approached him, though, perhaps disgusted by his grotesque appearance and stench, or maybe due to the strange circumstances through which he'd arrived.

Their response made Jonah frown. Surprise, then disbelief, crossed his features.

Seeing his consternation, they repeated, "The port of Jaffa."

A wry smile appeared on Jonah's face. He was back where he had started.

In the Temple, which seemed so long ago now, he had received the command to go to Nineveh. His reaction had been to travel to Jaffa and escape to Tarshish. But his time in the fish and subsequent exit—which could be likened to the gestation period of a fetus and its birth—had released a new Jonah. He'd experienced a rebirth.

And this Jonah would heed the call and travel from Jaffa to Nineveh.

The curious onlookers started firing questions at him, so fast he could barely begin to stammer an answer. They inquired about his identity and his entrance into the fish, as well as the experience inside its belly and the ways he managed to survive.

There was no reply from Jonah. The crowd turned away from him, content to continue their exchange without his input. Murmurs of conversation reached his ears as he lay there. The fishermen were having difficulties coming to terms with what they'd seen.

One man's voice could be heard above the rest. "Every day, early in the morning, we arrive at the port. We don't leave until we fill our quota, whether that be enough fish to feed our families or a surplus to sell at market."

Those around him nodded their heads in assent. He continued, "We live and breathe our trade. We know it all, from the various types of fish to the best way to bait them, to how to gut them and how to sell them."

"Not to mention methods for cooking and preserving them," interrupted a robust woman, holding a bawling red-faced infant over her shoulder as she patted its back.

"Yes," he responded before turning back to the crowd to resume his address. "How did this happen? Every day we catch and eat fish, yet here we have encountered a giant fish that caught and swallowed—nay, ate a man."

His words sparked a debate, and several people started speaking at once. There was plenty of shouting, combined with remarks of outrage and disbelief, as they attempted to grasp the fact that they had just witnessed an inversion of their reality.

One bald man, stroking his long and bushy beard, asserted himself over the others. "It is a sign. This is an omen heralding the introduction of some change into our lives too. Once animals start changing their nature, anything can happen, all rules can be challenged."

His comments were met with a flurry of excitement as the crowd discussed the significance of the appearance of the giant fish.

Jonah tuned them all out. He was too tired to talk to them. He had more pressing needs: He had to eat, bathe and freshen himself up, and commence his mission as soon as possible. His lips were dry and swollen, painful to move. His mouth felt thick and furry with the accumulation of scum on his teeth and tongue.

He weighed his options and concluded that he would barter: some food for his story. He only required light fare—some water and crusts of bread or pieces of fruit. Nothing too heavy for his hollow stomach and dry throat. Just enough to hydrate himself and line his painfully empty innards.

Jonah sat up slowly and peered into the crowd. He was searching for something in particular, though he couldn't necessarily say what. He would know it when he found it.

Then he found her. A shy child peering out from behind the robes of a short, fairly nondescript fisherman, who presumably, by the way she was clutching onto him, was her father. Alert hazel eyes gazed at him from a chubby face almost hidden behind a mass of dark ringlets.

Jonah beckoned to her and asked for some food. She looked to her father for permission, and after receiving a nod, she ran off. She returned just a few minutes later with some meager provisions and sat down as near to him as her round scrunched-up nose would permit.

Once he had rinsed his hands and mouth and uttered thanks to God, he gulped down some water and began to tear into the hunks of bread. He turned the pieces over in his mouth, enjoying the texture and savoring the crunchy burned parts. The feel of something filling his mouth, being able to chew and gnaw with his teeth, was such an intense pleasure that the staleness of the bread was immaterial.

The surrounding group looked on in fascination as this disheveled man savored the scraps of food. It looked like he hadn't eaten in days.

After a few minutes focused solely on mastication, he was ready to share pieces of his story with the crowd of onlookers. He began with the crux of the whole thing; there was no point in leading in gently. After all, they had just watched a fish spit him out. He doubted he could shock them any further.

In a matter-of-fact tone, he relayed that he was the prophet Jonah and that he had been running from God to avoid delivering a prophecy to Nineveh. He shared with them the details of how he'd failed in his attempt to flee from God. Jonah described how God had caused a great storm directly over his ship, leaving the rest of the sea clear and peaceful.

He chose not to divulge that the sailors had been apologetic and reluctant to throw him overboard. That even after a confession and a lottery that deemed him responsible for the supernatural conditions, the sailors had tried to row back to shore in an attempt to save his life. Their sensitivity had come as a surprise to him; he wasn't sure what to make of it. It was not a point on which he wanted to dwell.

He recounted being thrown overboard, the sensation of drowning, being so close to death and then getting swallowed by a large fish that had housed him for three days. He touched upon some of the physical details of being in the stomach of such a being but couldn't bring himself to speak of the mental anguish. Then he mentioned the death of the fish, as well as its resurrection.

The final event was his ejection, not just a means of being removed from the fish, but an additional brutal ordeal for his body as he was forced upward and outward. Even to Jonah's ears the tale sounded too fanciful and bizarre to be true.

It took the innocence and clarity of youth to really delve deep into the heart of the matter. The small curly-haired girl who had helped feed Jonah shyly posed a question that made everyone pause and Jonah smile in delight. "What does this mean for Dagon?"

Dagon was a popular god of fertility and grain. The top half of the idol was formed in the shape of a man, and from the navel downward it was fashioned as a fish. It was all too clear to those present that the god Dagon had been used as a tool by the God of Jonah, the God of the Israelites. Their gods paled in comparison to Him. This God was clearly such a superior force and might that not even Dagon could compete with He who could thwart nature for His own purpose.

Jonah's lips were now less swollen and cracked, and his stomach was somewhat sated. He realized it wouldn't be wise to put any more food or drink into his body in his malnourished and dehydrated state. No longer feeling quite as weak, he allowed his thoughts to stray from his physical health and to muse over the conversation taking place adjacent to him.

Amidst the commotion, a group of women in the middle of washing their laundry had abandoned their linens, leaving them scattered in disarray, to join the discussion. One lady cleared her throat to gain the attention of the crowd as she questioned the obvious symbolic connection to Nineveh.

"What does it mean," she asked in a voice full of drama, "that a fish brought this man—a man who was running from the city of Nineveh, a city known as 'the house of fish?'"

Jonah, who had tried to escape Nineveh—the great city of three days' walk, a busy trade city famously symbolized by a fish within a house—had been housed in a great fish for three days. Of course, that made sense. One thing that had been inherently obvious to Jonah during his time in the fish was that he could not evade God nor his mission.

Word spread about the great fish, as well as the news that Jonah was back. Friends, fellow merchants, and supporters of the man of God emerged from the crowd to greet him and look after him. They gathered around him, gingerly helping him up off the dirt.

As Jonah placed his feet on the ground, he jerked from the pain. His bright-red, blistered skin felt sore and sensitive from his ordeal in the fish. He wobbled, almost losing his balance. His muscles were weak from disuse. One friend wanted to carry him, but Jonah insisted on walking. Men positioned themselves on either side of him to support him.

Jonah inched forward, flinching each time his feet made contact with the hard surface. The gravel and stones scraped at the flaky, peeling skin on the soles of his feet, stinging him repeatedly, but he pushed the pain out of his mind, forcing himself onward.

They brought him to a medic not far from the port. This man supplied him with a bitter herbal tincture to help with the pain.

The medic and his assistant bathed Jonah and cleaned his injuries, rubbing in ointments to heal the chemical burns and oils to soften his skin. Jonah winced in agony every time they touched his skin, but he endured the suffering in silence. They bandaged his wounds and dressed him in clean clothing.

After an overnight stay, Jonah was impatient to get moving. His friends and colleagues tried to convince him to remain there longer, to give himself time to heal. They wanted to send for Shoshana to lift his spirits and take care of him.

But Jonah wouldn't hear of it. This was his chance to do the right thing, and he was eager to proceed with his travels. There could be no more delays. He needed to get to Nineveh.

Chapter 13

Nineveh

Jonah traveled by donkey along well-trodden paths, stopping only when his need for food or rest became urgent. Like a donkey that needs to be nudged onto the right path every time it turns astray, he too felt the hand of God guiding and steering him on the path to complete his mission.

As he approached Nineveh, he felt a need to continue the journey on foot. The walk wasn't easy. His legs felt weary and heavy. He trudged on as if he were wading through water, fighting against the waves.

He blocked out all physical sensations and just focused on keeping his limbs moving. He barely paid attention to the change in landscape, as the red-brown earthy dunes became lush grassy hills with an abundance of foliage.

At one point, he felt a splash of liquid on the underside of his wrist, looked down, and discovered that he was holding a flask full of water. Someone must have given it to him, although who it was, he could not recall. He eagerly gulped it down, enjoying the refreshing sensation of the dampness sliding down his parched throat.

It was ironic. Once, he had so desperately and eagerly chased after prophecy, and now that he was the one delivering prophecy, he would do anything to escape it.

He cast his mind back to one particular episode in his childhood. It had been a cold, gray, wintry morning when he'd looked on enviously as his father prepared to leave for a few days to convey a prophecy. Young Jonah desperately wanted to accompany him. He watched his father pack a small bag of essentials, including some homemade food lovingly prepared by Jonah's mother.

Acting on impulse, Jonah had haphazardly tossed some of his own belongings into a sack and ran out, chasing after his father. He wanted to be with him; he wanted to share in the prophetic revelation. He longed to be a prophet like his father. His father had been amused, chuckling at the sight of his small son dragging an oversized bag behind him. Lifting him onto his shoulders, he had carried Jonah home, gently chiding him for running away.

Be careful what you wish for, Jonah thought wryly.

Jonah may have been oblivious to his surroundings as he approached Nineveh, but his eyes took in everything as he reached the tall and imposing walls surrounding the city. In front of him were enormous wooden gates that towered over him. One gate was open wide; the other one was shut tight.

He very much doubted the closure was a method to control the ebb and flow of passage into the city, since there was a strong military presence equipped to deal with crowd control. No, this gate was closed so that the artwork could be admired. Depictions of warfare were engraved on the bronze bands decorating the cedar gates. Assyrian soldiers burning bodies, flaying them alive, torturing their victims with cruel and unspeakable horrors. These gates were used to ensure that all those who entered Nineveh, the capital of Assyria, would be intimidated; to impress upon visitors exactly with whom they were dealing.

Looking around, it was easy to identify who, like himself, was new to Nineveh. They were the people who stopped and stared at the gates, wide-eyed, with open mouths. Jonah saw faces full of admiration for these brave, victorious warriors, as well as others who looked sickened by the way the Assyrians mistreated those weaker than themselves—maybe even fearful that they could easily find themselves on the receiving end of such atrocities.

Jonah moved closer to the gate, mesmerized by the images. Those in front of him moved aside so he could step closer. With his sore hands and ragged fingernails, he traced the carved pictures of slaves tearing out their hair in mourning, women begging for mercy, and vultures circling in the air.

His head swam as visions from his prophecies of the Assyrian soldiers attacking the Northern Kingdom merged with the images in front of him: archers aiming, stones flying through the air, flaming torches, chariots trampling people, soldiers carrying the heads of their enemies, wagons filled with booty, cattle, and slaves. He gasped in horror at the barbaric pictures, and with that intake of air, he returned to reality.

Then, without allowing himself further thought, he stepped through the gates of Nineveh.

Numb to the world, he just focused on putting one foot in front of the other. He had to keep moving. He didn't want to be here, but he had no choice. This task had been thrust upon him, and him alone. This large city, this vast mission, everything around him was so large and overwhelming, so beyond him. The heaviness of his task made his shoulders curl inward and his back hunch over. The responsibility literally weighed him down.

What if he failed? He contemplated a scenario where his words would elicit no reaction and Nineveh would continue along the same path. Was that, in fact, success? Perhaps failure in his eyes was that he would invoke change, and then God would have mercy on the city. He was fearful of failure and yet fearful of success at the same time. No matter the outcome, he couldn't win. He had another pang of longing for his home, his wife, and the life he had left behind.

He continued on his way. At one point, he paused and peered over his shoulder to see how far he'd come. He stood there, looking back, the tails of his robe extending out into the wind like a cape. To his great surprise, there were hordes of people traipsing after him.

To an outsider, he gave the impression of an army general leading his troops. He saw the way some of them were looking at him, full of hope. He heard snatches of conversation from those nearby. Snippets here and there, enough to know that they were talking about him, admiring him. They seemed to be expecting something from him. What did he have to give them?

There was an air of jubilation and anticipation among his followers. Jonah didn't actively encourage their company; he walked a distance in front of them, aloof and alone. He wasn't interested in mixing or conversing with them; he was in a world of his own.

He knew he had reached the right place as soon as his sensitive olfactory system picked up the strong odors associated with a crowded area: rotten garbage, human sweat, pungent cuisine, and other undefined fumes. The stench of a built-up and heavily populated area clogged his pores. The cacophony of shouting voices from those purveying their wares and haggling over prices filled his ears. His nose twitched, and his eyes watered at the foreign scents and perfumes assaulting his senses.

In front of him lay a bustling marketplace, a landscape of colors: chains of beads in vivid blues arranged beside swatches of textiles, terra-cotta pottery in ruddy browns, bouquets of herbs in hues of greens dangling from a thick rope. The scent of hyssop wafted toward him. Spices in various shades lay spread out like an artist's palette, and a fine mustard-yellow powder caught his attention with its vibrant color.

There were dried fruits glistening, and nuts in beiges and browns arranged to invite perusal, although beady-eyed merchants guarded their products against the hands of those unwilling to pay for their fancy. Several bedraggled children stood around, trying to appear nonchalant as they waited for the right time to pounce; a moment of distraction was all these skilled opportunists needed.

Jonah stopped. This point of commerce and social activity was an ideal place. He spotted a wooden platform nearby. Besides some rolls of material lying discarded to one side, it was otherwise fairly clean and clear; most importantly, it was centrally located.

Using his upper body strength, he strained to pull himself up onto this makeshift stage. The exertion was too much for him, and he was left dangling for several minutes as his muscles gave out. He tried to recover his breath as he hung suspended in midair, feeling like he was in limbo, neither here nor there. He continued his efforts, panting and puffing, until he finally pulled himself onto the planks.

Jonah waited for the crowd to catch up with him. He paused and took a deep breath, trying not to inhale the foul surrounding environment, and struggling to draw inner peace and calm from within. He wanted to distance himself from this foreign place. The sooner he began, the sooner he could finish.

The people stilled, turning to look at him. There was a low murmur as those present wondered who he was and what he was doing there.

From high up on the platform, he gazed down at the populace surrounding him. He swallowed the bile rising from his stomach, and in a loud voice that seemed to echo and ring out in all the neighboring lands, he declared, "Forty days—Nineveh is overturned."

Five words. A short prophecy. He wanted to be as brief, concise, and to the point as possible. He didn't feel like elaborating or persuading the people to repent, but he was under compulsion to deliver God's word to them. This was him fulfilling his requirement in the most laconic way possible.

There was an expectant air as the people waited for him to continue. A few long moments of silence passed until it became clear that he had finished. During that lengthy, pregnant pause, he glanced around at the gathered people of Nineveh.

He didn't want to initiate eye contact with them. He couldn't bear to look at them, yet one old man shuffling to his left caught his gaze. Thoughts consumed him, flooding his consciousness.

Have those cold green eyes witnessed affliction and theft? Has that crooked nose pointed in the air as you looked on at those suffering? Are those wrinkles and lines around your mouth formed from smirking and jeering at the people you cheated? Has your hair turned silver-gray because of the guilt you felt for robbing them?

Then he turned his attention to a young mother standing directly in front of him. Her brood was gathered close to her. An infant, swaddled tightly in a protective gesture, was pinned to her chest, a toddler was tied to her back by a swath of brown cloth, and two young children clutched either side of her long, flowing skirt.

He couldn't help but wonder which of these children, grandchildren, or future generations would be the ones to march against the Israelites in the Northern Kingdom; to destroy, plunder, and pillage the Jewish land, exiling and scattering its inhabitants to other lands.

In their quest for power, these seemingly innocent children could one day execute great cruelty against many nations, including the people of Israel, destroying and carrying off babes just like the ones in front of him.

Chapter 14

Nineveh's Response

He had spoken only a handful of words, yet they caused a considerable commotion.

Those present who had heard Jonah's message quickly relayed it to everyone else.

"A fast day!" declared a loud, high-pitched cry. Other voices chimed in to agree with the sentiment and to repeat the phrase.

The marketplace was startled into action as merchants responded by packing up their stalls and halting their sales. Linen sheets were thrown over the produce to cover it. Nuts and seeds were spilled on the ground in the scramble to hide them away. The air was thick with the scents of herbs and perfume as petals and leaves flew about and were crushed underfoot in the stampede.

There was the sound of pottery smashing and shards scattering as a large earthenware vase shattered in a stall owner's hastiness to bundle his merchandise out of sight.

Sacks were grabbed from piles and handed out to all those within reach, who hurriedly donned them. Those who didn't receive sackcloth ripped their own clothing instead and began to moan and wail.

Jonah was stung by their response. He couldn't fathom what he was seeing. The city's inhabitants were actually listening—men and women, old and young alike. With astonishing speed, they were attempting to distance themselves from their previous actions. He hadn't had to convince them with long speeches and rhetoric, let alone resort to begging them. All it had taken were five words, and, somehow, the city seemed to be overturning itself in an effort to repent.

This was a far cry from his experience with the Israelite people, which generally involved them laughing and jeering at him. Some ignored him. Many times, he had been told to go away and take his religious messages to the temples. A few individuals jested with him about how much money he was paid to do his job. Sometimes, the insults were more menacing, and the crowds threw things at him, like rotten fruit. Jonah shuddered as he remembered one such incident involving moldy figs being pelted at him. He had detested the sight and taste of figs for months afterward.

The Israelites preferred to listen to the false prophets who delivered positive, encouraging, and generic messages about how well they were faring and how they should continue on with their current behavior. In Jonah's experience, few people liked to be told that they were wrong or imperfect or in need of some change.

Yet the people of Nineveh seemed open to hearing this truth and prepared to change.

Word carried swiftly to the palace. The king had already been informed of the existence and appearance of this Jonah figure. His network of spies and messengers was extensive, and he was aware of most incidents and occurrences within his city. Now, he was updated with news of this short prophecy and the flurry of activity that was taking place in response.

With great surprise, he realized that the visitor must be the one about whom the Tarshish officials and sailors had spoken. Apparently, he hadn't been murdered after all—or perhaps he'd been resurrected? Who knew the power of this God?

Being a levelheaded and intelligent individual, the king did not go into a panic over Jonah's message. Instead, he mulled over the words. These five words gave him pause. Actually, they provided him with the hope of salvation.

He had picked up on the not-so-subtle references to the societies of Noah and Sodom, which had been destroyed by this God in the past. The forty days they were being given to change their ways was reminiscent of the forty days of the Flood in the time of Noah. Only, this time the period of forty days was in advance of the punishment. Surely, that indicated the possibility of a chance to repent and change.

"Overturned," the word used to describe their possible punishment, prompted thoughts of the overturning of Sodom. Though Nineveh was, like Sodom, guilty of sins of theft, violence, and immorality, he would convince the people to reform their ways.

He was already somewhat familiar with the God of Jonah and the Israelite people. There was still talk of the miracles in Egypt from long ago. The priests spoke with awe about the ten plagues released on the Egyptian people while the neighboring Israelites were unaffected: Blood in the River Nile, being overrun by frogs, infected with lice, and an invasion of wild animals, the death of their livestock, an outbreak of boils, hailstones raining down on them, swarms of locusts, thick paralyzing darkness, and the death of the firstborn males.

There were tales of the splitting of the sea too, resulting in the drowning of the entire Egyptian army. Pharaoh hadn't listened to this God—and look how things had ended for him and his nation. This was a powerful God, and if the king were to save his city, he needed to convince the people to repent and change their ways.

Starting with himself.

He had the palace closed off to the public, shutting the huge doors to the entrance and posting extra guards outside to ensure those inside weren't disturbed. The king held a private meeting with his team of advisors. It didn't take long for them to draft a strategy. It was clear what action needed to be taken, and that it must be done immediately.

Satisfied with their unanimous decisions, he pushed aside his footstool and rose from his elaborate bronze throne. He discarded his scepter, and it fell to the ground, knocking against the legs of the throne, which were shaped like a lion's paws.

The priest sprinkled his head with some holy water while chanting a blessing to grant him help and success from the gods. Then, the king left his sword, bow, and quiver with his courtiers and strode down the corridor to his private chamber.

His valet, an elderly man with graying hair who had been with him since he was a baby, helped to strip away the layers of his royal robes. The rich maroon and crimson fabrics fell crumpled to the floor, resembling a pool of blood. He pulled the beige sackcloth over his own head and tugged it down. The cheap material felt rough and coarse against his pampered skin.

His attendant removed most of his jewelry, including his rosette bracelet. A sprinkling of ashes left a charcoal smudge on his forehead, making his thin black brows stand bolder and more defined.

Even in his hurry, the king, clad in sackcloth, couldn't help but notice the contrast between his current simple, modest attire and the decadence of his palace. The ostentatiousness glared at him; the gold, ivory, and lapis lazuli laid into the furniture. The colors in the wall relief seemed blindingly bright, with scenes from violent military campaigns depicted in great and lurid detail.

As he made his way along the corridor to the palace entrance, he passed eunuchs swatting flies and spraying perfume, and musicians playing the lyre. His bare feet looked out of place against the ornate patterns of the limestone floor.

Servants were situated all over the palace with trays of refreshments, ever ready to serve the royal family. One man held out a gold drinking vessel, proudly displaying the detailed carving of a ferocious lion's head. A tall serving girl offered the king a bunch of red grapes, each one as large as a date. On second glance, she was actually very short in stature but appeared far taller due to the braids she had pinned on top of her head in an elaborate hairstyle.

In disgust, the king knocked the tray, spilling its contents. He shouted at his servants, "No food! Fast! Repent!" The silver tray sent a loud crashing noise reverberating through the palace as it hit the floor.

At the entrance to the palace, the king's armed guards stood near the huge, imposing statues flanking the doorway. With his own head, the wings of an eagle, and the body of a bull, these colossal statues, known as Lamassu, ensured that the spirits protected him. He wondered if these spirits would be of any use against the God he now faced.

The royal chariot raced from the palace to the marketplace. Jonah, who had failed to rise to action when told to do so by God, the King of the universe, bitterly noted the alacrity with which this human king launched into action.

The king stepped out of the chariot and was carried onto the same platform that Jonah had stood on not long before. Murmurs broke out among the crowd gathered as they expressed shock at seeing their usually extravagant king appear before them in such simplicity and humility. Messengers on horseback situated themselves around the marketplace, waiting impatiently to ride off and spread the king's message across the city.

The market had been silent as the people had listened to the words of Jonah. Now again there was a state of hushed quiet as they waited for the king's speech.

With an air of confidence and determination, he addressed his people. "Neither food nor water should be consumed by person or animal," he said. Pinching his sackcloth between his fingers, he instructed, "All must wear sackcloth and cry out in prayer to God. Who knows whether God will turn away from His anger so we shall not perish?"

He wasn't declaring anything new; his subjects had already accepted these very same impositions on themselves. However, they were in awe of their leader. He was clearly practicing what he preached. Besides this, he was renowned for his intelligence and proficiency in giving counsel.

Hearing his royal proclamation sent the people into a fresh fit of fervor as they clamored to show their sincerity.

Jonah wanted—no, needed—to escape. He was feeling suffocated among the crowd of miscreants. He couldn't seem to get away from the people fast enough. He knew that he should appreciate or even admire the actions of the king. His noble example encouraged his people. Unlike the last king he had visited, King Jeroboam II, this monarch actually seemed to be listening to God.

Yet all it did for Jonah was to rouse feelings of annoyance and agitation. It didn't help that the king reminded him so much of the ship's captain. Both were far too hasty in their transformation, and Jonah didn't doubt that both would be quick to revert to their old ways again too.

There was another person in the crowd who couldn't help but draw a comparison between the king and the captain. Both were strong and muscular men, but otherwise, physically, they had little in common. The captain was tall and strapping, an imposing figure with a bald head, dark beard, and swarthy, weathered skin from his time at sea.

The king's brown skin was supple, having been protected from the elements. His dark locks flowed freely down his back like a majestic crown and cape all in one. His beard was elaborately braided. His bright-blue eyes matched the sapphire ring on his smooth, manicured fingers. Even clad in sackcloth, he managed to look regal.

Despite their differences, these two men radiated an air of leadership, leaving their mark on those in their sphere of influence. Both were charismatic leaders who inspired men to follow them.

The fellow in the crowd had good reason to compare these two, for he was one of very few present, besides Jonah, who knew both the captain as well as the king.

He had been a sailor on the way to Tarshish on that fateful voyage.

His heart had almost ceased beating when he'd seen Jonah climb onto the timber platform. He recognized him, not from the rumors swarming like locusts, but from his personal experience on board the ship with him.

A ghost. A dead man returned. He thought he would faint with shock. Feeling anxious, he'd bitten down on the soft pink flesh of his inner cheek. He'd tried to slow his rapid breath. He was willing to bet all his wages that this was the same voyager, and when the confident baritone echoed across the square, he knew it with certainty.

They had watched him drown. They had waited for some kind of miracle, for him to rise up and reappear from the waters. After a while, they were forced to admit that he was gone. How could he explain that he was seeing this man again? Had he risen from the dead? His once-luxurious robes were unrecognizable, but the way he carried himself couldn't be mistaken. His skin appeared raw, burned and scarred. His face, never plump to begin with, was now gaunt, full of sharp angles like shards of glass. With the hollowing of his cheekbones, his eyes had become even more piercing, like rays of the sun ready to burn whatever they met.

He couldn't help but notice that Jonah didn't smile. He looked depressed and dejected, and he tried to avoid eye contact with the people of Nineveh. Such an exalted figure, his mere presence could motivate the people, yet it looked like he couldn't bear to be around them. It was a perplexing thought for the sailor, but one that was washed away quickly by his disbelief at the sight in front of him.

He still couldn't believe the voyager was actually here. His mind couldn't comprehend the reality of what his eyes were seeing. How could the man be alive? How was it physically possible?

These questions demanded answers, but the sailor's heart won over his head. He was overcome with emotion and gratitude that this man was alive and overwhelmed by the power and might of God. Tears of relief streamed down his face at the realization that they hadn't, in fact, murdered this man of God.

As the sailor marveled at this great miracle, his mouth arched upward into a smile. The mysterious voyager must have come to help them change for the better, he concluded. He dropped to his knees in appreciation and thanks to God.

Chapter 15

Nineveh Repents

With his job over, Jonah intended to make a hasty exit. Freed of his burden and constraints, his legs, heavy and resistant throughout his one-day walk across Nineveh, now felt light and agile.

An old lady, bent over and walking with difficulty, stopped him in his path.

With a toothless grin, she presented him with her offerings. After murmuring a thanks to her and a blessing to the Lord, he accepted a tall earthenware jug from her outstretched, wrinkled hands. He thirstily drank some goat's milk. He took a waterskin and a handful of almonds and dried grapes for the way, stuffing them in a fold in his clothes as he hurried down the hill away from this terrible city.

It was a dirty, unsightly, and congested place. As if to confirm his words, a gust of wind blew, bringing with it a handful of dust and rocks from a nearby building site. It was hard to miss the construction that was taking place all over Nineveh.

Also prevalent throughout the land were the heavily armed groups of soldiers, loud and boisterous as they strutted around. Their military presence reminded Jonah of what the future could bring if the Assyrians would invade the Northern Kingdom. It only served to propel him faster in his eagerness to leave the place.

Only one day earlier, the people of Nineveh had been engaging in all sorts of foul behaviors. Then, suddenly, a transformation had taken place. Just a handful of words, and they were all seemingly spurred to reject their previous ways.

"Please!" Jonah mocked aloud. "As if anyone could be taken in by their act." Jonah found the whole proceedings ludicrous, bizarre even. It was like a theater performance, some kind of comedy. The speed with which it had taken place was abnormal. Their organization and efficiency made Jonah feel as if this were some kind of stunt they pulled every so often.

And didn't it bother anyone else that the poor animals were forced to participate in the repentance? Dressed up in sackcloth and ashes like their owners, it was as if they too had engaged in sin. Livestock were forced to fast, with no food or liquid passing their lips. He had witnessed female animals being forcibly separated from their young sucklings, so that the animals would call out in hunger and pain. These people were committing acts of cruelty and had somehow convinced themselves that this was for their betterment. It was shocking, not to mention crooked.

He had seen people engaged in what appeared to be acts of repentance. They returned stolen objects to their neighbors and friends with downcast eyes and apologies. He saw one man dismantle his entire house, brick by brick, in order to find a particular beam he had stolen from a neighbor which he needed to return.

The whole thing was farcical; he could have just repaid the cost or replaced it with another beam. It looked wonderful on the outside, he conceded, but he wondered how many stolen goods were still hidden away within his home, safely concealed in drawers and safes. He was dubious of their intentions and was sure it was just a show. Utterly ridiculous. A city of hypocrites.

What use was it when the fabric of society had already been eroded. A tapestry once rich in intricate detail, woven with skill, had been slowly worn away. The knots had been purposefully frayed, holes had been created, and pieces had been cut out. Cheating, deception, swindling and theft had all torn away at the threads. This was nothing anyone would notice on a day-to-day basis; it had happened slowly, right under their eyes. Then, one day, the piece of art and beauty was suddenly more emptiness than togetherness. Where bonds and connections should have been built, family life had been torn apart, causing social decay. The whole community suffered. Nineveh was too far gone to be repaired.

Such intense emotions swirled within him—anger, sadness, fury, and loneliness. His feelings were so strong that he couldn't contain them all. They threatened to spill over, battling inside him to escape. He wanted to strike out at someone or something, like Moses with the rock. He picked up some pebbles lying in his path and skimmed them across the ground as far away as they would scatter.

He threw his arms heavenward and tilted his head back so that he could gaze up at the clear sky. He opened his mouth wide and screamed with a primal rage.

Why was he suffering so much? If anyone should be suffering, it should be the people of Nineveh. He wasn't the bad one. He wasn't an idolater, a man of violence who took what he wanted, cheated, bullied, or spoke vulgar, coarse language.

"I knew it; I knew this was going to happen. This is why I ran away to Tarshish in the first place." Jonah paced back and forth, hands clasped behind his back as he addressed God. He was speaking with confidence, self-assurance, and anger. It didn't occur to him to trust God or ask Him to explain His reasoning.

Verses from chapter 34 of Exodus spouted from his lips. Words that had worked for Moses, many years prior, when he'd begged for communal forgiveness after the sin of the golden calf.

"God of compassion, mercy, slow to anger, and abundant in kindness, who regrets evil." As Jonah articulated God's attributes, using the words Moses spoke to overcome God's wrath, he found his own anger increasing. Ironically, he was using a prayer typically recited to request Divine mercy in order to criticize God's use of mercy.

He deliberately left out one key element from the prayer: the attribute of being truthful. It was in the original composition, and it stood out now, stark in its absence. He found its inclusion to be a lie. Jonah, a man of *emet*, a just and uncompromising fellow with strong principles, could not deal with this lack of truth. He didn't want to be in a world with a merciful God, an inconsistent God. How could it be right or true for sinners to be so readily forgiven?

Perhaps if he paused to think, to examine things more objectively, he would realize that he had inverted reality so that he saw mercy as evil and death as good. But Jonah was too preoccupied and consumed with his anger. "Take my soul. Better that I should die, God. I am willing for my life to end; I cannot live in a world like this, a world that lacks truth. Just as good deeds should be rewarded, bad acts should be punished."

The sailor who had recognized Jonah wandered after him, trailing after the prophet across the city. At first, he hoped to catch up with him and touch his shoulder, feel his flesh, and be reassured that he really was alive. He was also looking for a word of recognition or some encouragement and inspiration from this sage.

Then, as he saw the alacrity with which Jonah almost ran out of Nineveh, he chased after him out of curiosity. What matter of importance could be waiting for him that would cause him to hurry from Nineveh? He resolved to follow; he had accompanied him on a voyage at sea, now he would join him for this journey on land.

The sailor stood out of sight. Jonah seemed so caught up in himself and his emotions that it was unlikely the prophet would have spotted him anyway. It wasn't so much that he was trying to hide, more that he just wasn't certain that an intrusion would be welcomed at this time. He didn't know what to make of the strange things he was witnessing. In his limited interaction with Jonah on the boat, he had seemed a calm and composed man, confident of his choices even when those around him were flailing. Now that the people of Nineveh had resolved to become better people, Jonah seemed to be the one flailing.

Just the thought of the people of Nineveh filled him with admiration. They'd been given a deadline of forty days, and they hadn't even needed to use it. Their response had been immediate. It was remarkable how much they had achieved in such a short time—not only the speed with which it was accomplished, but also the process and outcome.

God couldn't fail to appreciate the transformation. These external changes in their apparel and actions surely reflected their deep desire to change their inner being as well. The entire society had been involved—from the greatest among them, the king, down to the children and even the animals.

The sailor had wandered around the city, admiring the fervor and diligence with which people were behaving. He witnessed a farmer separating his cows from their nursing young. He saw this emotional scene repeated several times that day, and each time it brought tears to his eyes. The farmers left the barns, their arms filled with the squirming, grunting calves upset at being taken from their mothers.

Hearing the pitiful cries of those animals longing to feed and be fed was heart-wrenching. The mothers could be heard bellowing from within the barn, desperate to be reunited with their young. The consensus was that these cries would elicit pity, encouraging even the most hardened hearts to melt and repent, and, of course, would encourage the Israelite God to feel compassion for them too.

Another noteworthy act he witnessed was the dismantling of a home. The very same scene that disgusted Jonah left the sailor in awe. Watching in amazement, he saw a short, stocky man pull his house apart to return materials stolen from his neighbors.

In the weeks since he had abandoned life at sea, the sailor had found work as a laborer. Building gardens, walls, towers, and palaces wasn't as adventurous as sailing the high seas. It also lacked the comradeship and close bonds formed by sailors living and working in close, cramped quarters for months at a time. But he was accustomed to physical labor, and there was plenty of work available with all the construction going on in the vibrant metropolis of Nineveh.

With his recent involvement in the construction trade, he could truly appreciate the enormity of this act. It was an enormous undertaking to destroy a home and then rebuild it from scratch.

He had proposed a simpler and easier solution: to offer compensation instead. But the homeowner wouldn't hear of it. The man barely stopped his work to respond to the sailor, just pausing long enough to blurt out that he couldn't stand the idea of living in a home built on thievery. Instead, he planned to destroy the foundations and rebuild his home—and his morals—anew.

The sailor had been awestruck. The way the people of Nineveh were turning their lives around was so impressive.

Kikayon

J onah roamed the area in search of large leaves, sticks, and fallen tree branches. The lack of vegetation meant that it took him some time to find what he needed. Selecting some of the taller, stronger branches from his collection, he planted them into the ground. Firmly, he pushed the last one deep into the sand, then released his hold on it to test its stability.

Sweat coated his back, and he wiped his forehead with a corner of his sleeve. Cupping his hand on his brow, he shielded his eyes from the sunlight. The sun was burning overhead, and the work of building himself a shelter—a sukkah—was taxing. He threw some large palm leaves over the top of the poles to create a roof and provide himself with some shade, then moved inside the booth.

Jonah sighed at the instant relief it provided him, particularly his skin, even now sore and sensitive from his time in the fish. The epidermis was still peeling off his arms, exposing red and tender skin beneath.

Sitting in his shelter, Jonah was struck by the irony that this entire saga had all begun with a sukkah too. His visit to the Temple over Sukkot had given him such immense joy, enabling him to receive the prophecy regarding Nineveh.

Not just a sukkah, he thought, as he tipped his flask upside down to get out the last few drops of water. It had all begun with the water-drawing ceremony. Water was such a precious commodity; his livelihood relied on water. He had traveled through raging waters on a boat and in a fish. Water, so essential and yet so simple.

Throughout the year, wine libations are offered on the altar in the Temple—wine, aged and refined, just like the elite among the Jewish people. Water, on the other hand, represents the average person. Just like with the four species, so many aspects of Sukkot celebrate the importance of each individual. Not just every individual, but each nation too. During the week of Sukkot, seventy sacrifices are offered up in the Temple, one for each of the seventy nations of the world, as the Israelite nation is deeply concerned with the welfare of the entire world.

Day after day, Jonah sat reveling in the shade. With little else to occupy his attention, he allowed his imagination to run free. He envisaged the scene taking place behind him—fountains of red-hot molten lava springing up from the midst of Nineveh; the earth split open with wide fissures; buildings and homes toppled over; debris spilling all over the streets.

Gripped by a mixture of anticipation, dread, and excitement, he slowly turned around to see what lay behind him. He almost expected to turn into a pillar of salt, like Lot's wife. No scene out of Sodom and Gomorrah greeted his eyes, though. It was a silent nothing. The landscape and architecture were intact, and there was no fire or brimstone. The skies were a clear blue, barely a cloud in sight, let alone hailstones.

Nineveh had not been overturned; it had not been destroyed. It had been left untouched.

Maybe it hadn't happened yet. Not all forty days had passed. There was still time for raging waters to flood Nineveh and submerge the city, drowning all its inhabitants, Jonah thought. A scowl overshadowed his face at the lack of consequences that the city had incurred. He sat watching for several hours in the hope that something would change, but besides the sand scattering in the breeze and the lizards scuttling across the desert floor, all was still.

The stillness was broken by a bird fluttering overhead. As it dived closer, Jonah realized with a start that it was a dove. This was no coincidence; how could it be, when his own name, Jonah, meant a dove?

As his hand trailed across the sand, sifting coarse grains between his fingers, he let his mind wander. What was going on here? He could sense the Divine plan, the broader scheme. He recognized that he was but a brushstroke on a canvas, a single thread in a woven wall hanging.

He wasn't the first dove who'd been dispatched to deliver a message.

Jonah mulled over the similarities between his current situation and that of Noah's, long ago.

After the great Flood, Noah had sent out a dove from the ark to check on the water level—not once, but twice. So too, Jonah had been thrown off the boat into the water, and twice commanded to go to Nineveh.

But that's where the similarities ended. Noah's dove had faithfully fulfilled his mission and returned to the ark. Jonah hadn't been as quick to obey God. It had taken him a while to complete his mission and return to God.

There were other disparities too. Back then the Flood had lasted forty days. Here, forty days had been given as a warning before the punishment was even to take place. More importantly, both groups of people had sinned, but this time no destruction had occurred.

The sailor continued to watch Jonah, half amused by the sight of this grown man protesting and complaining. But it was also frightening to watch an adult battle an invisible adversary. Jonah ranted and raved, paced, and tore at his clothing.

Then, in an instant, he seemed to deflate, like an empty bag, its contents used up and the bag itself just a barren container. Jonah collapsed in a heap, sending dust scattering as his body dropped to the floor. He began weeping long and hard. His moans and cries were so loud, so painful, that the sailor had to cover his ears. He couldn't bear to see this great man reduced to such a pitiful state.

"So unjust," Jonah mumbled repeatedly. There may have been other words or phrases thrown in as well, but they were unintelligible, incoherent. A once jovial, energetic, groomed figure who walked around with confidence, Jonah was reduced to a shell of his former self. He was now a gaunt, depressed man. He seemed to have shrunk in stature. He was tired of life, lackluster and dull like tarnished silver.

The sailor felt uncomfortable with this invasion of Jonah's privacy, but he didn't budge. He remained there, on the side, observing him. At one point he contemplated getting involved. He stepped forward, about to move closer and go to Jonah's aid, to talk to him, hold him, soothe him even. But at the last minute he hesitated and lost the courage.

FOR DAYS JONAH RESTED THERE, watching and waiting. The booth he had built was starting to dry out. He wasn't sure how much longer it would last. The wood was becoming brittle, and the leaves were deteriorating. It still provided some protection from the bright sun, but not enough, as evidenced by his throbbing headache.

His mental exertion and the lack of food and drink didn't help either. He nibbled on the few nuts and pieces of dried fruit he had left, sucking the sweetness and enjoying the moisture. He pressed his knuckles to his forehead to try and lessen the pain. He massaged the bone above his brow, close to his eye sockets; the pressure awarded him some temporary relief. He longed for some water and an herbal tincture right now.

But sleep was what he needed most. Hopefully, upon awaking, the pain would be gone.

When he opened his eyes again, he glanced about and was struck by something new that had appeared in the bleak landscape. There seemed to be a patch of greenery, a new plant just outside his shelter. A broad grin lit up his face.

He jumped up and ran out to check what he was seeing. A tall kikayon bush had sprung up. There had been no sign of life in this area; it was a barren patch of land. No seeds had been planted, and yet, this plant had sprouted. It was a miracle, a gift from God, and it made his heart sing with joy.

Looking at the bush was a source of absolute jubilation for Jonah. Not too long before, he had been angry and morose; now his spirits were lifted. The world hadn't changed, but he felt that everywhere he looked was covered in a warm glow. His whole perspective had changed. His cloud, the thick gray thunderstorm that had been hanging over his head, was gone, blown away, replaced with sunshine. Life looked so positive. He could taste the goodness in the back of his throat, a sweet and wholesome flavor.

He could barely contain his immense happiness. He wept with joy. Tears fell in rivulets down his face, washing away the grime and leaving a salty residue on the tip of his tongue. Spontaneous laughter erupted from within him. His legs started to jig, and he danced on the spot.

Words of praise flowed freely from his mouth. *"Hodu la'Hashem ki tov*—Thank you God, for He is good."

HE WAS STILL CHUCKLING when he sat down under the bush. The leafy bush that towered over him was such a comforting sight. It was proof that God was thinking about him, caring for him, and loving him. He was alive, and the earth was alive with possibility. Optimism filled him. With the grace of God, his fortunes had changed. He'd been on the brink of disaster, and here hope had come out of nowhere.

He plucked a few of the leaves and rubbed them between his fingers. He brought them to his nose, inhaling the fresh and light aroma. He even placed one on his tongue. He let it sit, savoring the crispness before it seemed to melt in his mouth. Immediately, it refreshed and energized him; perhaps it had medicinal properties.

His aches and ailments were eased, his pain diminished, and his body felt strong again. He took in the state of his feet, bruised and battered but starting to heal. He looked down wistfully at his tattered rags; once, he had been dressed in his best robes, selected especially for the Temple visit. He ran a hand through his hair, catching it in the matted strands and knots. Goodness knew what kind of bird's nest his beard resembled.

This attire and appearance were unusual for him. His life was so completely out of routine—such a contrast to this bushy tree standing over him, solid and reliable, stable and permanent. A tree is planted for the future, with the intention to provide fruit and shelter for years to come, for subsequent generations. He felt a momentary pang for all that he had left behind, for Shoshana and for the family he lacked and might never have. His own trees back home would outlive him, though who knew who they would serve.

THE SAILOR MUST HAVE DOZED OFF in the heat. He didn't even realize he was napping until he was shocked into wakefulness. His body was sore and uncomfortable from falling asleep in a strange position. He had pins and needles in his left leg, and his neck and shoulders were stiff. He massaged his leg and rolled his shoulders to ease his muscles.

Something had awoken him. *What was that noise?* There had been some kind of disturbance, perhaps an attack or a wild animal? Bewildered, he looked around and saw that it was coming from Jonah.

He'd watched Jonah go to sleep morose and depressed. Now, the prophet was carefree and exuberant, emitting squeals of delight. The source of his jubilation was obvious: a large shrub or tree of some sort with what looked like gourds growing on it. Miraculously, it seemed to have appeared out of thin air.

The shrub was providing Jonah with some extra shade. Definitely helpful, but was it really so exciting? For a man saved from drowning and delivered by a fish, it was perplexing that this vegetation could be the cause of such an outpouring of praise to God. His behavior was overly dramatic, absurd even. Was it all because of a plant that had only just appeared? As he watched an elated Jonah spend the day basking in the shade of the plant, the sailor tried to work out what benefit he was overlooking.

Chapter 17

The Worm

Jonah must have succumbed to sleep at some point in the night. He awoke after a deep and satisfying slumber. He felt groggy and rubbed his eyes, shaking his head to dispel some of the weariness. With his eyelids still closed, he yawned. His mouth stretched open wide, like a nestling opening its beak to accept food from its mother. He opened his eyes with a smile and a heartfelt prayer on his lips, ready to welcome the new day.

He noticed immediately that something was off and stood up with a start.

His beautiful plant—his gift from heaven—was gone.

No, not completely gone. It was still there, but no longer majestic and tall, no longer sheltering Jonah in his booth. Instead, it lay shriveled, crumpled in a heap. A single small white worm was wiggling around its roots, burrowing in them. Seemingly, this small worm had conquered the huge plant.

Despair overcame Jonah as he looked at the withered kikayon plant.

Suddenly, out of nowhere, a strong gale swept his way, the likes of which he hadn't felt since the storm on the boat. Bereft of the plant's shelter, the full force hit Jonah, knocking him off balance. A violent gust of wind tore at him, trying to rip off what remained of his cloak. He felt exposed as it clawed at his skin. It attacked his orifices, working its way into any opening it could find and causing him excruciating pain.

The noise deafened him. He slammed the palms of his hands over his ears to try and protect them and quell his suffering. As the wind pounded against him, trying to wear him down, the burning rays of the sun joined the battle. He was being attacked on all fronts. He curled up into himself to limit his exposure to the wind and sun.

Anger filled his bones, causing his muscles to tense and his teeth to clench. He was incensed that God would take this kikayon from him. He had only enjoyed it for a short time, just one day. Why had it been taken from him? Why were all good things being snatched from him?

He thought fleetingly of his wife. He wondered where she was now, what she was doing. He ached to be with her and return to the simple life they lived. What he would give to see her smile again, hear her laugh. Their future had been pulled out from under their feet, like one of the rugs she wove.

Needing something to divert his pain and anguish, he turned his attention to the culprit. He stared at the worm. It seemed to grow larger before his very eyes, until it began to resemble the treacherous snake from the Garden of Eden that had brought downfall to the world.

Jonah again felt ready to die. *But God won't give me that satisfaction*, he thought bitterly. He was in such a state of melancholy as he faced yet another low in his life. He wanted to give up; he wanted out. Some part of him knew that this wasn't the answer, but he was struggling so much. He felt so alone.

He couldn't even turn to God anymore, not when he struggled to relate to His sense of justice or truth. Where did that leave him? He didn't want a God who was so kind and generous. He didn't want to live in the world as it was. Jonah believed the world required consistency and consequences, and he couldn't accept the allowances God was making.

Robbed of a shelter, the scorching heat of the merciless sun enervated him to the point of collapse. He slumped to the floor in a faint.

God's voice came to him, "Are you so angry about the kikayon?"

Jonah felt like Adam in the garden of Eden being asked a question to which God already knew the answer. It was plain to see that he was furious. "So angry!" he shouted. "Without the kikayon in my life anymore, I want to die." Of course, it wasn't just the physical loss of the kikayon; it was the loss of all that it symbolized.

"Jonah," God's voice continued, "you pitied the kikayon, yet you didn't make it or contribute to it. It appeared overnight, and now, a day later, it disappeared. Yet here you are, complaining and wanting to die due to its loss. Shouldn't I have pity on Nineveh, this great city of more than twelve thousand people, who don't know their left from their right, and also their cattle?"

Pity them? What about pity for Jonah? Greatness had been thrust on him. The huge task he'd been forced to undertake had burdened him. It wasn't something he had sought. If anything, he had fled from it. He would much rather have stayed home. Jonah's love and loyalty lay with the people of Israel; they were his concern. They needed him. Enough was going on with his own people within his own land. Why couldn't he be with them, persuading them to repent?

Numerous and ignorant: that was a good way to sum up the undeserving people of Nineveh. However, Jonah couldn't help but notice that God had made no mention of Nineveh's repentance. Was it because they lacked sincerity? Or perhaps because their repentance would be short-lived, like the kikayon?

Then again, though the plant had been around for just a day, it had existed long enough to provide value, to make a difference to Jonah. Could it be that the repentance of Nineveh, though fleeting and temporal, was still worthwhile? Or could it be that God loved them regardless? Was it possible that He loved them simply because they existed, notwithstanding their actions and even their morality?

Or was the opportunity to repent not even offered on their own merit? Had the people of Nineveh been saved only because of the righteous conduct of their founder, Ashur, who built the city to move his children away from the negative influence of Nimrod? These were troubling thoughts.

THE SAILOR LOOKED ON with astonishment. He was struggling to comprehend what was taking place in front of him—the fast-growing plant, the worm, and the extreme weather conditions. It was incredible to observe.

And he couldn't fathom Jonah's radical reactions. All he could see was the love and care God had for this individual. God had been involved with Jonah for the entire sea voyage, and underwater too. His presence had been clearly felt in Nineveh, where Jonah's success had been swift and smooth.

Now, in the desert, the sailor had watched a miraculous plant grow and then wither. By the time he felt the strong wind and scorching sun, he was staggered by the extent of God's supervision and involvement in Jonah's life; He was directing so many forces of nature for the sake of one individual. Being a spectator was such a humbling and powerful religious experience for the sailor.

The sailor had seen so much change occur: on the boat, in Nineveh, within himself, and within nature. Yet it seemed that Jonah hadn't changed, despite everything he'd gone through. He was the agent of change, yet he remained unchanged. Even the animals had overcome their nature and were transformed. Didn't Jonah realize the trail of Godliness he'd left in his wake? He'd never bothered to look back to see or enjoy it, never even realizing there was anything behind him. A wave of sadness and disillusionment washed over the sailor.

He continued to watch Jonah, curious about his next moves. Jonah remained seated inside what remained of his collapsing booth. The external structure seemed reflective of his deteriorating internal state. What, if anything, would happen next? Jonah continued to sit in meditation, unconsciously playing with the *tarshish* stone around his neck. His back was ramrod straight; the rigidity of his posture appeared not so different from the inflexibility of his beliefs.

Then something totally unexpected happened. Jonah stood up and left the booth, suddenly coming face-to-face with the sailor.

Startled, Jonah gaped at him, at first unable to comprehend that another person was present in this deserted area. Then recognition flashed across his face, and with a smile he asked, "Aren't you...?"

Before Jonah could complete the sentence, the sailor finished it for him. "The sailor from the ship, from that stormy trip? Yes, yes, I am. I was one of those who threw you overboard."

The two of them stared at each other for several long moments. The sailor grew increasingly uncomfortable and started to shuffle his feet. Without thinking, his hand rubbed his earlobe, reaching for the sun and moon charms that had once hung from his gold hoop. It was a habit borne out of a lifetime of praying to the gods of the sun and moon. He was still adjusting to the absence of his earring, removed after his previous encounter with Jonah aboard the ship.

The sailor was mustering the courage to speak up and apologize for his presence, but Jonah acted first. He threw his arms around the sailor in a tight embrace. "My friend," he said, "I am going home to see my wife, but first I am stopping at the Temple in Jerusalem to pay my vows. Perhaps you would like to join me?"

Author's Notes

We are told of a prophet from the Northern Kingdom, called Jonah the son of Amitai, who visited King Jeroboam II, son of Jehoash, to deliver the message of the expansion of Israel's Northern borders (Kings II 14:25). He ruled for about one hundred years before the exile of the ten tribes, approximately the eighth century BCE. His reign was a time of economic prosperity, but also idolatry, corruption, and social injustice.

It seems that Jonah lived a very long life, over 120 years, according to the book *Seder Olam Rabbah*. This would explain how he lived during the reign of Jeroboam II, the fourteenth king of Israel, as well as the reign of King Ahab. Ahab reigned when Jonah was a young boy, the son of the widow of Zarephath, brought back to life by the prophet Elijah. Then, Elijah's successor, Elisha, sent the young prophet Jonah to secretly anoint Jehu as the next king of Israel (*Rashi* on Kings II 9:1).

Chapter 1

Jonah received his prophecy at the Temple, during Sukkot, the Festival of Tabernacles, at a *Simchat Beit HaShoeivah*, a water-drawing ceremony.

The Spirit of God only comes upon a person when they are in a state of joy (Jerusalem Talmud *Sukkah* 5:1). "One who did not see the *Simchat Beit HaShoeivah* in his life never saw true rejoicing (*Sukkah* 5:1)."

There is no reference to Jonah's wife or children—if he had any—in the Book of Jonah. We learn of the existence of his wife from a Talmudic discussion over whether women can undertake optional rites. The wife of Jonah is one of the examples offered. She undertook the pilgrimage to bring sacrifices, even though she was not obligated to do so (*Eruvin* 96a).

The custom of tying a golden thread around the four species was common practice in Jerusalem after Jonah's lifetime (*Sukkah* 36b). So too, the Midrashic source outlining how each of the four species (the palm branch, myrtle, willow, and etrog) represent different levels of wisdom and Torah observance is recorded after Jonah's time. It is possible, however, that this practice, as well as the understanding of the four species, were known to Jonah during his lifetime (Midrash *Vayikra Rabbah* 30:12). The midrash details that the palm branch, edible with no smell, is likened to a person with wisdom but no good deeds. With its fine fragrance but no taste, the myrtle represents a person with good deeds but lacking in wisdom. The willow has neither fragrance nor taste, symbolizing the one with neither good deeds nor Torah learning; and the etrog, with its fine taste and fragrance, represents a person with both. On Sukkot these four species must be gathered and united, just as the Jewish people are interconnected and each person needs to be tolerated and included in the nation.

A comparison is drawn between the three prophets: Jonah, Moses, and Jeremiah. Moses and Jeremiah also refused to accept their God-given missions. However, their refusals were out of a sense of humility and not feeling suitable for the position, not because they disagreed with it (*Shemot Rabbah* 4:3).

Jonah thought that he would not receive prophecy outside the land of Israel (*Radak* 1:3). A prophet who suppresses his prophecy receives the death penalty (*Sanhedrin* 89a). *Malbim* (1:2) disagrees that Jonah suppressed it, since he had not yet fully received the prophecy. *Malbim* says Jonah had been called by God but was not given the specific details until he was spat out of the fish. The *Radvaz* agrees, also offering the possibility that Jonah may still have been a novice prophet and that sometimes a new prophet may not fully comprehend a prophecy.

Chapter 2

Why didn't Jonah want to go to Nineveh?

- Should the inhabitants of Nineveh repent, it would reflect badly on the Israelite people, who hadn't listened to the many prophets sent to rebuke them (*Radak* 1:1).

- Jonah would be seen as a false prophet when the people of Nineveh repented and his words wouldn't be fulfilled (*Rashi* 4:1).
- In the future, Assyria would attack the Israelites and exile the ten tribes. Jonah didn't want to save the very people who would harm the Israelite people (*Malbim* 1:2; Kings II 17:6–8). He preferred to suffer, and even die, in order to protect the Israelite people.
- Jonah's devotion to truth, *emet*, and justice meant that he wanted punishment for the people of Nineveh. To him, the idea of repentance seemed unjust. He didn't want to see them treated with mercy and awarded the chance to repent.

Chapter 3

Jonah clearly wanted to go to Tarshish; it is mentioned three times in the text. There are several ideas about where Tarshish was located: Tarsus, Turkey, or Spain. It was a remote place that had not heard of God (Isaiah 66:19). It was a land of great wealth. It had gold, silver, ivory, apes, and peacocks (Ezekiel 27:12 and Kings I 10:22).

There is a debate over which tribe Jonah was from, Asher or Zebulun. The resolution is that Jonah's father, Amitai, was from the tribe of Zebulun, and his mother from the tribe of Asher (Jerusalem Talmud *Sukkah* 5:1). Tarshish is also the name of a precious stone, one of which was on the breastplate of the High Priest of the Temple (Exodus 28:20). The Targum suggests it is a stone associated with the color of the ocean. Interestingly enough, it is debated whether this stone represents Asher or Zebulun (first heard from Gitta Neufeld on yutorah.org and later read in an article by Rav Yehudah Shaviv in the Yeshivat Har Etzion weekly newsletter, 770).

Chapter 4

Kings II (14:25) records that Jonah the son of Amitai was from Gat Hefer. This is in the Northern Kingdom, part of the land designated for the tribe of Zebulun (Joshua 19:13).

Chapter 5

Amos was a contemporary of Jonah. His main activity was in the Northern Kingdom. He prophesied about the execution of members of the house of Jeroboam II and the destruction of their temples (Amos 7:9).

Chapter 6

In Genesis (49:13), Jacob blesses his son Zebulun to dwell near the sea and be involved in maritime trade.

Jonah wanted a boat to Tarshish, and then one appeared. He took this as a sign that he was doing the correct thing (*Pirkei D'Rabi Eliezer* 10:1).

A rocking boat filled with sailors of ill-repute leads to less favorable conditions for prophecy (*Malbim* on Jonah 1:3).

There was a gradual transition from Akkadian to Aramaic in the Neo-Assyrian era, so the sailors on the boat to Tarshish, as well as the people of Nineveh, may have spoken Akkadian or Aramaic.

Tarshish was known for its magnificent ships (Isaiah 2:16).

Prophets are wealthy. According to some, it is a requirement for becoming a prophet; others say it is a consequence of being a prophet. Usually, fares were paid at the end of a journey. It was unusual that Jonah paid in advance. Also, he paid for the entire ship, not just the fare for his own passage (*Rashi* 1:3). According to *Nedarim* (38a), this fare was four thousand gold dinars.

The sailors came from all the nations of the world and spoke all seventy languages, representing the seventy nations of the world and a microcosm of the world (*Pirkei D'Rabi Eliezer* 10:4).

Chapter 7

The sailors asked what Jonah's profession was, as they assumed he was a thief or swindler (*Radak* on Jonah 1:8).

There had been a previous storm that returned these sailors, who were already two days' distance from Jaffa, back to Jaffa (*Yalkut Shimoni* on *Nach* 550; *Pirkei D'Rabi Eliezer* 10:1).

The storm on Jonah's ship came after one day of travel (*Pirkei D'Rabi Eliezer* 10:3).

According to the text, Jonah didn't immediately go to sleep; he only did so once the cargo had been thrown overboard, meaning he must have had some idea of the severity of the storm. I followed the approach of *Daat Mikra* on Jonah (p. 5, note 21), which suggests that he went down to sleep earlier, before the storm began.

Rav Shlomo Aviner, in his commentary, *Book of Yonah* (p. 46), offers two different ideas as to why Jonah went straight to sleep. The first, according to Rabbeinu Bachya, is that he was confident that he was acting correctly. He also brings the opinion of the *Radal* on *Pirkei D'Rabi Eliezer* (chapter 10) that Jonah fell asleep out of distress and shame, and his sleep was thus a form of escape.

Chapter 8

On p. 15 of her book, *Jonah, The Reluctant Prophet*, Dr. Erica Brown writes that with one word—*Ivri*—"he covered his profession, his people, and his country. This one word, *Ivri*, suggests a transitional identity. *La'avor* is "to cross over"; an *ivri* is one who crosses over. Jonah was a crosser, one who used to be one thing and then, through a transformative act, became another. The king "took off"—*vaya'aver* (3:6)—his robe when transitioning from royalty to penitent. But the same root word also conveys the notion of sin. An *aveirah* is a transgression; one might cross the line, so to speak, or break through an acceptable boundary."

The lots were done using small stones (*Daat Mikra* p. 16). During Jonah's lifetime, the people were deeply superstitious. It wouldn't have been unusual to carry around lottery equipment to help them make decisions. They conducted their lotteries ritually, in the presence of their idols.

Chapter 9

The Midrash gives a favorable impression of the sailors who were so reluctant to throw Jonah overboard. First they cast Jonah into the sea up to his knees, until the storm abated. Then they picked him up, and the storm resumed. They lowered him again, this time until his navel, and the waters stilled, until they lifted him out again. They then lowered him until his neck, and again the waters abated. When they lifted him up, the storm resumed with a furious pace, so they threw him in, and the storm ended (*Pirkei D'Rabi Eliezer* 10:6).

Chapter 10

In 1:16, the sailors offered sacrifices and made vows. The sacrifices, according to the *Radak*, were not done immediately while on the boat. *Metzudat David* says that they decided they would bring a sacrifice to the Temple. According to the *Radak*, the vows were promises such as giving charity to the poor. According to *Rashi*, they converted to Judaism.

One of my favorite sources (*Ibn Ezra* on Jonah 3:3, also mentioned in *Radak* 3:5) explains that information from the sailors reached the city in advance. The sailors arrived in Nineveh and told the people about Jonah, which is why the people of Nineveh so readily believed Jonah when they met him. In following this opinion, I faced the difficulty of constructing a realistic timeline. Jonah is in the fish for three days, but it is highly unlikely the sailors would have made it to Nineveh that fast. They also couldn't sail to Nineveh, as it is accessed from the River Tigris, not the Mediterranean Sea. Dr. Raphael Zarum shared with me his view that Jonah could have been spat out in Jaffa, restarting his aborted mission. This also accounts for the parallels and similar language of 1:1–2 and 3:1–2.

It is plausible that Tarshish would have been part of the Assyrian Empire—if Assyria was an empire at the time. However, Assyria may just have been a strong power at the time, becoming an empire only later on.

Nineveh was the capital of Assyria. This trade city was found on the eastern banks of the Tigris river, in the modern Iraqi city of Mosul. It was located at a significant intersection for commercial routes. It was an important highway for sailors and merchants. The cuneiform of Nineveh is a fish within a house. That fits the etymology of the name Nineveh, meaning "house/place of fish." The name seems to be derived from the Aramaic *nun* or *nuna*, denoting fish. This could be due to the abundance of fish in the river Tigris. It could also be connected to the Akkadian *nina* or *ninua*, which may have referred to their patron goddess. *Nina* was one of the Babylonian names for the goddess Ishtar (Brown, *Jonah, The Reluctant Prophet*, pp. 121–122).

The storm only affected their boat; the waters were calm and peaceful for the surrounding waters and ships (Midrash, *Pirkei D'Rabi Eliezer* 10:3, and *Rashi* on 1:7).

Chapter 11

The sun burned Jonah's skin, which was already sensitive from having been in the fish (*Ibn Ezra* 4:6).

The word "fish" changes from *dag* (2:1) to *dagah* (2:2). The most commonly known explanation is the *Mechilta* quoted by *Rashi* (*Jonah* 2:1), which explains that Jonah was in a male fish, but it was too comfortable, so he was spat out and swallowed by a pregnant fish. There, because of all the roe, he was uncomfortable and forced to pray. Another explanation is that it was a large fish (*dag*) that spat him into a smaller fish (*dagah*) (*Nedarim* 51b). A third opinion is that it was a live fish (*dag*) that then died (*dagah*). (Thanks to Rabbi Dr. Meir Levin of torah.org for his series "Yonah: Flight, Return, and Redemption." He introduced me to this *Rabbeinu Bachya* on Numbers 11:5). All the above opinions imply that Jonah's position became increasingly uncomfortable. The latter opinion also highlights the concept of mortality. (Also see *Zohar* on *Beshalach* 84–86. The fish died and was then revived and spat Jonah out in front of everyone.)

According to Yitzhak Berger (*Jonah in the Shadows of Eden*, p. 20), *dagah* is a reference to the story of the Israelites complaining about the manna in the desert. They longed to eat the fish, *dagah*, that they ate in Egypt for free (Numbers 11:5–6). "In the prophet's mind, the fish provides not a means to an end but an enduring, blissful escape analogous to the idyllic environs of Egypt."

Many Midrashim imply that being in the fish was a difficult and uncomfortable experience for Jonah. However, *Pirkei D'Rabi Eliezer* (10:8) offers an opinion that the fish was a loving, welcoming presence. The fish took Jonah on a tour, with its eyes acting as windows to the outside. It had a pearl hanging within to provide light.

The fish was created during the six days of creation to accomplish this task many years later (*Pirkei D'Rabi Eliezer* 10:7).

Jonah was the son of the widow of Zarephath, who sheltered Elijah in the time of Ahab (Kings I 17:9–24). The son died, and Elijah brought him back to life. The widow said that now she knew that Elijah spoke truth—*emet* (*Midrash Shochar Tov* 26:7).

Traditionally, if we are told the name of a prophet's father, it means that his father was also a prophet. Jonah was a student of Elijah and later Elisha (Kings II 9:1; see *Rashi* that the prophet who appointed King Jehu was Jonah).

Three prophets are described: Jeremiah, Elijah, and Jonah. Elijah is described as defending the honor of the Father (God). Jonah defended the son (i.e., the Israelite people) but not the Father. Jeremiah did both (*Mechilta D'Rabi Yishmael* 12:4).

It is unclear whether Jonah's prayer actually took place inside the fish or afterward. It seems that he was praying due to his difficult circumstances inside the fish and saved because of the prayer (*Ibn Ezra* 2:2). However, the prayer makes use of the past tense, so it seems as if he had already been saved. This could be because it is in the prophetic tense, where the past tense is used for future events that the prophet is confident will occur. Others hold that this prayer took place after he came out of the fish.

In his prayer, Jonah accused the sailors of making false promises that they wouldn't keep (*Radak* 2:9).

Chapter 12

Jonah's time in the fish was like the nine months a fetus spends in the womb, and it was as if he was reborn (*Malbim* 2:1).

Brown, in *Jonah, The Reluctant Prophet* (pp. 59–60), mentions that Dagon, a statue that was part man, part fish, was a popular god worshipped at that time. On p. 63 she talks about the inversion that takes place with the fish catching the man, rather than man fishing.

Chapter 13

The Balawat city gates are one of the highlights of the ancient Assyrian collection in the British Museum. Balawat was a city near to, and considered less important than, Nineveh. These wooden gates have strips of bronze mounted on them. These bronze bands have detailed reliefs showing scenes of warfare. In addition, one can see the colossal human-headed winged bulls, which flanked the principal rooms of the palace and were believed to act as guardians for spiritual protection. There are also carved stone panels detailed with images of archers, chariots, enemies being trampled, and vultures waiting to eat the carcasses.

All other details of Assyrian life are to my best efforts, details taken from tours of the British Museum and the Israel Museum. This includes mention and description of hairstyles and jewelry, in particular the rosette bracelet, as well as the mention of lions and the descriptions given of weapons, furniture, and decoration, including the royal drinking vessel and throne legs.

In *Jonah, The Reluctant Prophet*, Brown points out (p. xxiii) that "the word that appears with the greatest frequency in the book is *gadol* (great); it appears fourteen times in forty-eight verses."

Chapter 14

Radak (1:1) compares Jonah to the stories of Noach and Sodom. "Overturned" was used to describe the destruction of Sodom (Genesis 19:25, and Deuteronomy 29:22) and also for Nineveh (Jonah 3:4). The Flood lasted forty days (Genesis 7:4), and in Jonah forty days are mentioned (Jonah 3:4). Also, the sin in the times of the Flood was *chamas* (Genesis 6:11), often translated as violence, as is mentioned for Nineveh (Jonah 3:8).

According to the midrash, the king of Nineveh was once Pharaoh in Egypt. This cannot be taken literally, as the Book of Jonah occurred much later, but it highlights for us the many parallels between these stories (*Pirkei D'Rabi Eliezer* 43:8). One example of this is that the words "and they believed in God," appear both in the story of Jonah, in Jonah 3:5, and in the story of the Egyptians drowning, in Exodus 14:31.

The people readily listened to the king because of his sage advice, and the wisdom and counsel of his advisors (*Radak* 3:7).

There are many parallels between the captain of the ship and the king, for example, in the language they use ("*V'lo noved*—We shouldn't perish") (1:6 and 3:9; *Daat Mikra* on Jonah p. 15).

Chapter 15

The Babylonian Talmud (*Taanit* 16a) asserts that the repentance of Nineveh was genuine. It is used as a paradigm for how to behave on fast days. It details that if a house contained a stolen beam, they would tear down the whole house to return the beam. The Jerusalem Talmud

(2:1.13) disagrees, asserting that they returned what was visible but not the hidden treasures. Additionally, they used brazen tactics like starving their animals to force God to have mercy on them.

Chapter 16

A full comparison of the Jonah and Noah stories can be found in Judy Klitsner's book, *Subversive Sequels in the Bible*.

These ideas on water and wine are found on www.chabad.org in an article on Sukkot, based on teachings of the Lubavitcher Rebbe, entitled "The Taste of Water."

The kikayon is believed to be a fast-growing climbing plant with large leaves. According to *Ibn Ezra* (4:6), the kikayon is a gourd/pumpkin bush. Others say it is a plant from which castor oil is produced (*Radak* 4:6 and *Shabbat* 21a). Since the leaves on the castor oil plant are poisonous, I did not follow that interpretation but rather followed the words of Rabbah bar bar Chana that "under its branches rest all the sick of the West," implying medicinal qualities.

According to some sources, the kikayon was needed to provide shade for Jonah. This could be because the sukkah never provided total shade and protection in the first place, as it specifies that he sat "under the sukkah, in the shade" (*Malbim* 4:6). An alternative explanation suggests that the sukkah had dried up, so it no longer provided sufficient protection. The booth may have dried up from the heat of the sun (*Metzudat David* 4:6), or because forty days had already passed (*Radak* 4:6).

The ideas of the tree representing stability and permanence can be found on pp. 206–7 of Brown's book, *Jonah, The Reluctant Prophet*.

Chapter 17

This strong gale was deafening (*Ibn Ezra* 4:8).

Discussion on the comparison of the worm to the serpent of the Garden of Eden can be found on p. 15 of Yitzhak Berger's *Jonah in the Shadows of Eden*.

Nineveh was a city founded by Ashur after the Flood. This man was disgusted that his own children were acclaiming Nimrod as a deity instead of God, so he disassociated himself from Nimrod's kingdom and founded Ashur, known as Assyria. For this, the inhabitants of the capital, Nineveh, merited the warning of impending destruction (*Chizkuni,* Genesis 10:12).

The ending of the book of Jonah is inconclusive; we aren't given Jonah's response. We don't know if he changes after this experience. Did Jonah remain there, or did he return home? Did he visit the Temple (see p. 138 of Avigdor Shinan's *The Book of Jonah: A New Israeli Commentary*)? Did he continue as a prophet (*Yevamot* 98a)?

Glossary

Akkadian: an extinct language spoken in ancient Mesopotamia.

emet: the Hebrew term for truth.

etrog: a citron fruit.

four species: a bundle containing three types of branches—date palm, willow, and myrtle—used together with an etrog and waved in a special ceremony throughout the festival of Sukkot.

Game of Ur: otherwise known as the Game of Twenty Squares, this was a two-player board game that was popular in ancient Mesopotamia.

Lechem Hapanim: once a week twelve loaves of bread, called showbread, were baked and placed on the golden table in the Temple. Despite being left out for a week, these loaves did not go moldy or stale.

mikveh: ritual bath.

quppu ferry: a type of round boat traditionally used on the Tigris and Euphrates rivers in ancient Mesopotamia. The Akkadian word quppu means a basket, as these boats were woven from reeds and leaves and resembled a basket.

Simchat Beit HaShoeivah: the ceremony of water drawing. These were the festivities that took place each night during the week of Sukkot to celebrate drawing fresh water from the Shiloah spring and pouring it onto the altar in the Temple.

Sukkot: this week-long Jewish festival is one of the three pilgrimage festivals. It marks the end of the harvest time. It is celebrated by taking the four species as well as dwelling in huts. These temporary dwellings are referred to as "sukkot."

Torah: the first five books of the Hebrew bible.

Educator's Guide

Discussion Questions

1. How would you describe Jonah?
2. "This was no coincidence; how could it be, when his own name, Jonah, meant dove"? In Chapter 15, there is a reference to the meaning of Jonah's name. In the biblical book of Jonah, he is the only one given a name; the other characters are all anonymous. Why do you think this is? In *Jonah: House of Fish*, Jonah's wife is also given a name. What do you think about this choice? What do we see about the importance of names?
3. In what ways do you identify with Jonah?
4. What are the parallels between the captain of the ship and the king of Nineveh? What can we learn from them?
5. Besides the story of Noah and the Flood, what other biblical stories are hinted to in this story and the original text?
6. Why do you think the book of Jonah is read by Jews on Yom Kippur?
7. "Jonah syndrome/complex" is the fear of success and one's own greatness leading to the prevention of self-actualization. Have there been times in your life when you have experienced this?
8. Recurring topics in this book include: fire and water, Jonah's sandals, and weaving. Reflect on how these are used throughout the book.

Classroom Activities

1. Invite students, individually or with a partner, to write an alternative ending to this story. Students should use quotes from the text to explain their choice.

2. Visit the Assyrian collection of the British Museum, either in person or by taking a virtual tour. How does this enhance your students' understanding of the city of Nineveh and Jonah's fears?

3. Students should list all of the characters mentioned in the book, then choose one character and identify their traits and characteristics. Provide resources such as magazines and newspapers for students' use. Individually or as a group, students should select material to create a character collage. They should include quotes and descriptions from the book to demonstrate their understanding of this character.

4. Display artwork showing depictions of Jonah and the fish. Select images reflecting a range of interpretations of this biblical scene. Engage students in a discussion about the differences between the pictures. Have students draw their own version.

5. The book's preface ends with a quote by Abraham Joshua Heschel: "Jonah is running to Tarshish, whilst Nineveh is tottering on the brink. Are we not all guilty of Jonah's failure?" Students should research and select an up-to-date article referencing social injustice. Students need to write a summary of this current event to share with the class, as well as provide some practical ways in which the class can get involved, provide help, and take responsibility.

Bibliography

The following books have been of great help to me,
and I strongly recommend you add them to your reading list.

Aviner, Rav Shlomo. "Commentary on the Book of Yonah." Ateret.org.il.

Berger, Yitzhak. *Jonah in the Shadows of Eden*. Bloomington, Indianapolis: Indiana University Press, 2016.

Brown, Erica. *Jonah, The Reluctant Prophet*. Maggid Books, 2017.

Gesundheit, Benjamin. Studies on the Book of Yona (Hebrew). pp. 151–197 in *U'v'Yom Tzom Kippur Yeichateimu: Studies on Yom HaKippurim*. Edited by Amnon Bazak. Alon Shevut, Israel: Tevunot, 2004–5.

Klitsner, Judy. *Subversive Sequels in the Bible*: How biblical stories mine and undermine each other; chap. 1, pp.1–35. Maggid Books, 2019.

Leiman, Chaim Dov. *Our Lost Treasure*; chap. 16–17.

Mirasky, Meltzer and Keel, editors of *Daat Mikra*. Jerusalem: Mossad Harav Kook, 1990.

Shinan, Avigdor and Zakovitch, Yair. *The Book of Jonah, a New Israeli Commentary* (Hebrew), Tel Aviv: 2015.

About the Author

Ilana Harris is a writer and educator living in Jerusalem with her husband and five children. She has been involved in Jewish educational frameworks for many years, with a focus on pedagogy and Jewish texts. Her experience teaching in formal and informal programs in the UK and Israel led her to develop a creative approach that is inspiring, relevant, and thought-provoking. A graduate of Cambridge University, her further studies include an Educator's Fellowship in conjunction with the Hebrew University, as well as time in Midreshet Tehillah and Lindenbaum seminaries.

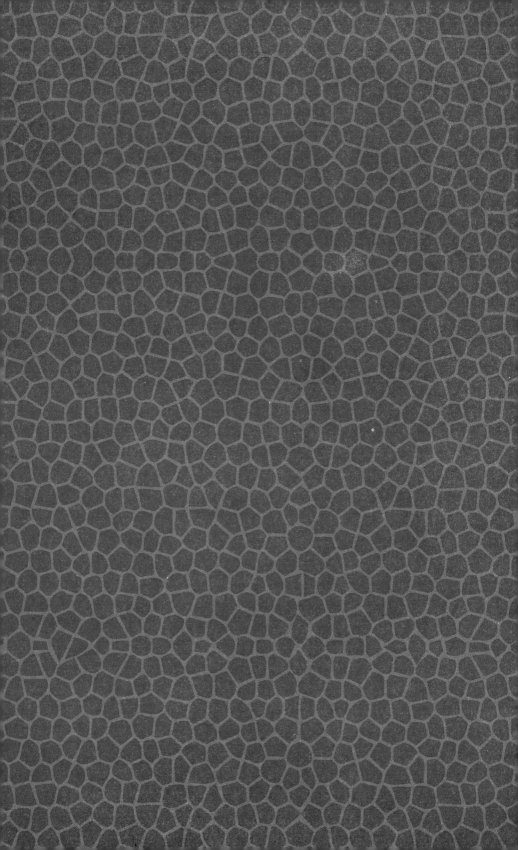